Hend and the Soldiers

MODERN MIDDLE EAST LITERATURES IN TRANSLATION SERIES

Hend and the Soldiers

a novel by BADRIAH ALBESHR

translated by SANNA DHAHIR

CENTER FOR MIDDLE EASTERN STUDIES

THE UNIVERSITY OF TEXAS AT AUSTIN

COVER IMAGE: Courtesy of iStock, ©ByeByeTokyo
SERIES EDITOR: Wendy E. Moore

LIBRARY OF CONGRESS CONTROL NUMBER: 2016962412
ISBN: 978-1-4773-1306-0

Originally published in Arabic as *Hend wa-l-'Askar* by Dar al-Saqi.
Badriah Albeshr © Dar al-Saqi, 2010, Nour Building, Oueini Street, Verdun,
Beirut, Lebanon.

Table of Contents

Introduction

Hend wa-l-'Askar (*Hend and the Soldiers*), by Saudi Arabian writer Badriah Albeshr, was published in Beirut, initially by Dar al-Adab (2006), then by Dar al-Saqi (2010). The novel appeared at a time when Saudi writers had recently started to speak openly about social issues their predecessors usually preferred to leave alone out of fear of retribution or reverence for social values. Not surprisingly, it was admired by all those who embraced its frankness, liberal views, and light, humorous tone; but it was equally attacked by religious groups and those who frowned upon seeing old traditions scoffed at or challenged. Like many other novels published in the Middle East during the first ten years of this century, such as Raja al-Sanea's *Girls of Riyadh* (2005), the novel was also perceived as a literary work whose author sought recognition or fast fame by introducing sexual and other anti-mainstream content. Although the novel was not banned in Saudi Arabia, it stirred such a controversy that Albeshr, when traveling to Kuwait in 2013 to attend a book fair, was prevented at the airport from entering the country.

The controversy surrounding the book was partly triggered by some passages that describe God in terms perceived as unprecedented in a Saudi novel. "In my mind," says the young Hend, "God assumed my mother's face, always angry, always threatening; the fire he promised was, on the whole, not much different from the pinches that her fingers burned on the insides of our tender thighs." This passage and similar others were used, usually out of context, to accuse the writer of blasphemy and of propagating immoral views. Furthermore, the novel's depiction of female sexuality offended those who called for due restraint in literary expressions. What especially fanned the flames of opposition were the scenes that present the Saudi religious police as hawkish figures, devoid of spirituality and humanity. And the novel's depiction of the jihadi and suicide bomber as the outcome of religious extremism and creeds that Albeshr describes as "muzzling the mind with fear" equally contributed to the campaign against the novel.

Yet despite the efforts to muddy its reputation, the novel has been described by the author as "the most popular" in her fictional oeuvre. This popularity is partly due to the growing number of open-minded individuals and groups in Saudi Arabia and the Gulf region that have mounted an opposition force to rigid religious politics. These include politicians and intellectuals, as well as a generation of young Saudis who have been exposed to other, more liberal, societies through the Internet and foreign travel. In his preface to the Arabic edition of Raja al-Sanea's novel, the Saudi liberal politician and well-known writer Ghazi al-Gosaibi speaks favorably of literature that addresses social issues with openness and sincerity. The Saudi literary scene has come a long way in this century; after decades of reluctance to disturb conventional mores, a number of female writers, including Raja Alem and Zainab Hifni, have become increasingly bolder in busting social taboos and lobbying for reform. Albeshr herself is aware of the new, progressive audience she is addressing: "not those who are set in their ways, but a younger, more open-minded generation."

Badriah Albeshr was born in Riyadh, in 1967, barely seven years after government education had been made available to Saudi girls. In a home where both parents were illiterate, the author feels greatly indebted to her older female relatives, especially her grandmother, for handing down a rare skill in oral narrative. In the mid-1980s, Albeshr went to King Saud University for a bachelor's, followed by a master's, in sociology. She started her writing career as a freelance journalist soon after obtaining her first degree, and by the early 1990s, she had established herself as a columnist in important newspapers such as *Al-Yamama* and *Al-Sharq al-Awsat*. Her career as a fiction writer also began during this period, with the publication of her first volume of short stories, *Nihayat al-Lu'ba* (Endgame, 1992), which was followed by the collections *Masa' al-Arbi'a'* (Wednesday Evening, 1996) and *Habbat al-Hal* (Cardamom Pod, 2000).

Her novels, *Hend wa-l-'Askar, Al-'Urjuha* (The Swing, 2010), and *Gharamiyyat Shari' al-A'sha* (Love Adventures in al-A'sha Street, 2013), came at a busy time in her life when she was teaching at a university in Dubai and publishing nonfiction works, such as *Ma'arik Tash Matash* (The Battles of *Tash Matash*, 2007) and *Najd Qabl al-Naft* (Najd before Oil, 2013). However, her teaching career, which followed the completion of her doctorate in sociology at the Lebanese University (2005), lasted until 2011, when Albeshr decided to dedicate herself to her writing. Albeshr is married to the famous comedy star Nassir Alqassabi, and the couple have successfully raised a family of three children.

The thought of translating this novel came to my mind soon after I finished reading it. I had been aware of the shortage of Saudi books in English translation, and I thought I should make Albeshr's novel available to English readers. It spans several decades of Saudi history and culture, all vividly portrayed through the eyes of a passionate insider. It would dispel a number of preconceived notions and fixed judgments about a people and many aspects of their lives in a place imperfectly understood by other cultures. Often these misconceptions have to do with women; this work, I thought, should contribute to setting them right. Here is a gallery of women who lead varied lives, defy all generalizations, challenge various coercive rules, and carve a niche for themselves against the odds. In the rigid society of this novel, men, too, rarely conform to prefigured images of men living in a strictly male-dominated world. In their variety and fluidity, they also defy gender stereotypes. Albeshr captures a post-oil, rapidly changing society in which past certainties are being constantly challenged, in which old traditions continue to be eroded, and portrays realities steadily embracing globalization.

The translation was not without its challenges. Besides having dissimilar structures, Arabic and English represent different cultures, the one can be very foreign to the other. These, however, weren't the hardest parts of the task. To render a readable and interesting target text, I set out to domesticate the translation in all parts that required idiomatic, clear English. At the same time, I strived to preserve the source text's local color, as in passages with religious sayings, salutations, and specific mannerisms. These, and some plays on words, which were often untranslatable, I sometimes transliterated and used footnotes to explain. Footnotes in fact were indispensable to clarity throughout the text. An important textual aspect I made sure to transfer to the English text is Albeshr's sense of humor, which required a lot of care on my part. The same is true of the poignant, moving scenes, especially in the novel's final section. Yet despite my vigilant eye, Arabic, my mother tongue, kept affirming its presence in the target text, in places where I least expected it. Therefore, I am grateful for the Western eyes that spotted and smoothed irregularities in the English text. One sincerely hopes that the present translation will be rewarding to its readers.

Hend and the Soldiers

One

DRAWING THE CURTAIN to one side, I looked out at the street facing my window. Children held their parents' hands as they walked along, and my ears picked up their voices. A yellow bus from the girls' school rumbled by, its young passengers draped in black abayas.[1] The next bus carried boys, who harried the driver with their screams.

The road celebrated the rain, asphalt playing games with the light, gentle spray, cooling itself from the heat of the sun on this early winter day.

My mother's voice urged little Mae to hurry up and get ready for school.

Birds clapped their wings in the sky, spreading their early-morning liveliness over the trees lining the pavement. Light drops of rain continued to fall gently to the ground.

The gates of dawn had set free a herd of clouds to graze the sky's azure meadows, and the sun wrapped itself in downy white sheets to rest. On the horizon, yet more ebullient clouds rose like steam from vessels in the sky, and young cloudlets bounced like happy soap bubbles.

When rain falls on the thirsty Najd,[2] people receive it with a frenzied joy. Najdi rain is by nature light and gentle and scarce. The smell of rain stirred the dried branches of my heart. It hurt to feel them breaking inside my ribs. As the parched leaves of memory fell, distant sorrows began to surface. My chest tight, I went in to wash myself before a short prayer.[3]

---

1. An outer garment, commonly black, worn by women in the Arab and Muslim world.
2. The name, which means "highlands," refers to the central regions of the Arabian Peninsula.
3. An optional two-genuflection prayer performed as Sunna (that is, according to the tradition of the Prophet Mohammed).

As I opened my bedroom door, the smell of coffee wafted from the kitchen; it spread throughout the house like fire on a hot summer day to greet my nose.

Ammousha, my mother's companion, roasts the coffee herself. She places the pale green beans in a hot frying pan and stirs them until they turn golden brown. The people of Najd do not like their coffee dark; they prefer it light brown, like a Bedouin's face tanned by the sun. Ammousha then lightly pounds the roasted beans into a coarse grind and throws a measure of it into the kettle. As the coffee begins to boil on the gentle flame of the stovetop, Ammousha adds half a measure of ground cardamom. Like a soul thirsty for union, the coffee clings to the soft particles of cardamom, smothering them with brown waves. The sweet smell of cardamom embraces the house as the mixture tosses and turns just before it boils over. Ammousha will not let it reach that point; she moves the pot away from the flame to give it a rest before returning it to the stove, where the frenzy begins again, lifting the cardamom to the surface in another cycle of rising and falling. After three boils and no more, Ammousha turns off the flame and removes the pot. The coffee settles down, swimming in the fragrant finished brew. The heady smell of cardamom penetrates our souls as we wait for our turn to drink the coffee and let it cleanse our morning moods, which are still entangled in the webs of the night's murky dreams. We luxuriate in it, expanding under the countless stories birthed by bitter coffee and sweet dates.

Most of the narratives in my life were spun during such coffee gatherings. Members of the group shed the fetters of everyday life and, after the third cup, proceed to tell their stories time and again, though never in the same way twice. Tales resist repeating themselves, and narrators do not wish to rely on the same details each time. In my family, the art of storytelling is passed down from generation to generation, though I was the first to commit stories to paper, having fondly listened until I developed the art of spinning them myself. I sometimes published them under a pseudonym. Initially it was a lack of confidence in my abilities that prevented me from using my real name, but later it was fear of the fury I was certain my stories would incite in my religious brother, Ibrahim, if he were to spot my real name in the papers. As it was, my writing caused several fights between the two of us, battles that only the story could win.

The histories of this household's women are tales woven around coffee. Each woman has a story living in the heart of her cup. If not given to her by fate, the woman herself creates a story to sweeten the acrid taste of life, and she relishes her own narrative over the bitter coffee. Each woman's tale emerges from the womb of a long cardamom pod, where her story had been growing.

Early one morning, Ammousha told me the story of my grandmother over a cup of coffee. It began with Abdul-Muhsin, my grandfather. He set out on a cold morning looking for his lost she-camel and came upon the slightly open door of Salem al-Dhal'an. He heard the pounding of a pestle breaking roasted coffee beans at the bottom of a mortar. The smell leaked out the door to where Abdul-Muhsin stood, vexed over the loss of his camel and longing for a cup of coffee to brighten his mood. He could not resist the smell, which slipped into every crevice of his mind. He knocked on the door.

"Salem!" he called.

"Welcome to you," responded Ibn Dhal'an. "Do come in!"

Abdul-Muhsin pulled the sides of his camel-hair cloak tight to warm himself against the cold. Warmth from the winter stove soon breathed into his body, which was excited by the smell of the coffee.

"Selma!" Ibn Dhal'an called to his daughter. "Bring us the cardamom."

Selma walked in wearing a green dress, her burka on her face and her narrow eyes flickering with a shy—though focused—look, which fell momentarily on Abdul-Muhsin. Black kohl framed her eyes, accentuating the spark of intelligence that even modesty could not extinguish. Her gaze planted itself on Abdul-Muhsin's susceptible, woman-loving heart; his mind had hardly anything to do with it. Selma's braid writhed like a long snake down her back as she walked; her full breasts were like two pomegranates under her green dress. She was tall and lean like a cardamom pod. At the door, she threw a bag toward her father and disappeared into the house. Abdul-Muhsin could hear her moving as he sat sipping his coffee. His troubled mood had all but vanished. Pleasurable sensations filled his soul and took him out of himself. It was as though another man, without his permission, were acting for him. Spreading out the wings of his cloak, he heard himself say, "Would you, Ibn Dhal'an, let me marry your daughter, Selma?"

Ibn Dhal'an was silent for a moment, stirring the coals on the hearth.

"I have no objection," he said. "Drink your coffee, and when you are finished, we will go to the sheikh to draw up a marriage contract."

His permission sent a jolt through Abdul-Muhsin, waking him up. He realized that he had put himself in a crazy situation, and he cursed the hour that led him to it. Today was no day for hunting gazelles, so why had he shot the first one that crossed his path? Abdul-Muhsin was known for his many marriages. He had been preparing himself for a hunt in faraway Hijaz the following day. Whenever he took such a long trip, he usually treated himself to a new wife. In Yanbu', where he went to trade, he had a wife named Safiyya, with whom he had three children; in al-Quds, a year before, he had married young Fatima, a merchant's daughter, who was anticipating a visit from him sometime this year; and in his house nearby, he had his wife Si'da, who would not for a minute believe this nonsense coffee story. This marriage would hold him back. He was about to set out on a long trip, hardly the time for adding a new wife to those he already had.

He was hoping that the sheikh would not be available so that he could escape a new marriage contract. No such luck. The sheikh was there and wedded him to Selma.

When his nearby wife heard about the marriage, she told anyone who would listen that Abdul-Muhsin had married Selma with no desire on his part. Unfortunately for her, the night her husband entered Selma's bridal chamber turned out to be the best he had ever experienced. Selma branded his heart with a passionate love that would not abate until the day of her death. She gave him two children: my mother, Heila,[4] and my uncle, Abdullah. After her death he continued to recite passionate poems that made those who listened feel he had never known another woman.

I had known Ammousha, a skinny black woman, since my childhood. Her small, keen, hawkish eyes were all we could see of her face, for she wore her burka all day long, even when she lay down to rest at noontime in the courtyard. When children saw her, they would take hold of it and try to pull it off her face, but she would gently slap their hands. "Leave my cover alone, boy!" she would say.

---

4. The name means "cardamom pod."

When she came to live with us after my father's death, she continued to wear her burka at all times. She would take her afternoon nap on the cushions placed on the living room floor, the burka draped on her face like a window shade pulled down for good, with its strings permanently tied behind her head. When little Mae ran around her, Ammousha would startle her from under her burka, making Mae believe she wore a mask in order to play a scary game with her. My mother would then reprimand Ammousha. "Raise your burka, Ammousha. You have frightened the little girl."

To which Ammousha would say, "I swear, sister, I can't see without it. It's like my eyes to me."

Later, she would gradually begin to lift it over her head, but only at certain times, and as soon as she heard a knock on the door or the voice of a man she would pull it down over her face again. "I feel naked without it," she would say.

We laughed when she said this, not knowing she did not intend her statement as a joke. But she was happy to have us laugh, and she lived and behaved spontaneously and with a light heart, unlike our mother, who thought one should not give in to gaiety and that women in particular should not raise their voices or laugh. In any case, Ammousha's features would momentarily surprise me whenever she uncovered her face. They were unusual: her small, flat nose; her wide, delicately structured mouth; and her yellow, coffee-stained teeth.

Ammousha was born in my ancestors' village in Najd, where my maternal grandparents, Abdul-Muhsin and Selma, were born. Her mother, Nweyyir, had come from another land, which Ammousha knew only through her mother's stories. I was seven when I met Ammousha's mother, a few years before she died; we had gone to attend a relative's wedding in the village. People called the blind woman Grandma Nweyyir, and I called her the same, not knowing why. It felt odd, but I heard the whole village, young and old, address her this way. She lived in a little house at the far end of the village, next to a well that was the center of many legends. According to people, one night a villager had been found suspended in the well by his loincloth. His howling had raised the whole village, bringing the men to his rescue.

Though she was blind, Nweyyir knew the way not only to her house but to every other house in the village. She walked alone with no guide but her cane tapping the roads and doors. The entire village, whose doors stood wide open to receive the sun as well as guests, welcomed Grandma Nweyyir; they were happy to hear her call out to them, her voice preceding her: "People of the house!"

Ammousha told me about the masked men who had kidnapped Nweyyir from the remote shores of Oman one day when she was seven years old. They carried her and many other children off and made them sleep in burlap bags at night for a whole month. During the day, the men hobbled the children's feet to stop them from running away. They fed them dry bread and water, sometimes adding shriveled dates to their diet. After many days of travel on the backs of camels, Nweyyir could no longer remember the voice of her pregnant mother, and her brothers' faces turned into painful images that choked her heart and halted the food in her throat. She soon began driving away memories of home in order to eat without pain. She also busied herself with work in order to forget. Yet every night her dreams would roam around her family's house and the village's spellbound well, tenanted by scorpions and jinn. Sometimes she thought she heard her father's voice singing on their roof terrace and the sounds of the games that she played with other children.

She was sold by coastal merchants to my paternal grandfather, Abdul-Rahman, who called her Nweyyir, a diminution of "Noura," erasing all traces of her Omani name. My grandfather used her as a slave for work, not as a concubine, and two years later married her to another slave who worked for him, named Jawhar, in order for her to bear him more slaves.

She had six sons and one daughter, Ammousha, who lived with the family and played with Abdul-Muhsin's children. Three of Nweyyir's sons died in the first half of the twentieth century during a bout of plague in the villages of Najd. Ammousha, a bony child, battled with death yet lived to be Nweyyir's eyes and the staff she leaned on to drive away the never-ending miseries of life.

Ammousha feared men. She told me about the pinch marks she often left on her daughters' thighs to stop them from going near them. "A man is like a dog," she would say. "He will drool at the mere sight of a woman, forgetting everything else."

I laughed at Ammousha's fears, which to me seemed grounded in low self-esteem. "Aunt Ammousha," I said to her, "I work with a lot of men at the hospital, and nothing untoward has happened to me."

"Not all of them are the same," she argued. "A woman may be plagued by a man who neither fears God nor is shamed by people's opinion."

"In that case, I'll know how to deal with him; I have an electric gadget that would freeze him right in his place."

She looked at me as though I had revealed a magic trick; then she thought I was making fun of her. She smiled, however, showing her black gums and yellow teeth, as she began to trust my words. "Truly, my daughter, today's girls are as scary as men."

One evening, when she was quite distressed, she told me about a young man, a neighbor of my grandfather, who had followed her to the fields of her "uncle"[5] Jab'an. All the men in the village were her uncles. She wouldn't dare oppose their will. Each had the right to hit her on the head, make a furtive pass at her, or slip his hand between her thighs. She would run away from their advances, being afraid of her mother, who would punish her when she complained about these insolent uncles.

She clearly remembered this young man, Obeid, who followed her. His being cross-eyed tricked her at first into believing he was not after her—there was no other way she could account for how she behaved that day, like a timid hen in the presence of a brazen cock. When she saw him she was halfway up a palm tree, picking a few fresh dates on that cool autumn afternoon. She did not know he had been stalking her, and his shadow in front of the tree filled her with terror. She realized immediately that this stalking would result in something dire. He sat at the foot of the tree, waiting for her. Sensing danger, she pleaded, "Move out of my way, Uncle; I may hurt you!"

"Don't be afraid; I'll help you," he said, his voice betraying his intentions.

"No, Uncle! No! Just move away," she insisted more firmly this time.

She would have continued as she was, stranded halfway up the palm tree, until this cross-eyed uncle decided to leave her alone, but the jagged

---

5. "Uncle" is a term of address used by slaves to show respect as well as servitude. "Aunt" is the feminine counterpart.

trunk poked into her foot and weakened her hold, causing her to slip and cut her knee against a stump. She fell bottom-first into the arms of Obeid, who pulled her to him, proving himself stronger than all her efforts to escape. She did not scream, afraid of being blamed by others. She might even be killed if they discovered what was happening to her. The imam of the mosque—who was always after her when she went into the mosque without a cover on her head—might issue an order for her death, which he himself would execute, his eyes red as live coals.

She tried again to plead with Obeid, keeping her voice low. "Uncle, I am your charge and your honor; my mother would cut my throat if she knew about this."

But Obeid would not listen; his bad eye rolled upward, showing white, as he held her breast and bit it. Of all her wounds from that day, the one on her knee, which took a whole month to heal, was clearest in her memory; she would bury Obeid's violations in the fathomless well of her fear and distrust of men. She could no longer remember how she got up that day and shook the dust off her dress.

Ammousha did not cry. She swallowed her tears as she reassured herself that, since no one saw or heard anything, she would not have to tell anyone or risk being punished. She didn't notice the red smears on the back of her dress, but her mother did while Ammousha was sleeping. She felt her mother's hands pulling her skirt down over her thighs and off her feet to wake her up and give her a lashing. Ammousha protested that she had done nothing wrong; it was Obeid, the animal, who would not let her breathe and then did what he did to her, which made the blood come down her thighs as well as from her injured knee.

"Uncle Obeid beat me," she said. "I'm a small girl. What else could I do?"

Ammousha married Fheid, a black shepherd who had been freed by Ibn Hamid. Fheid was a poor man who took care of the villagers' sheep for a meager fee. Ammousha complained about his laziness and abject poverty until her mother agreed to feed him as well as his family, instead of having him provide for them and meet their needs. Furthermore, each year he would add a new child to their household, for Ammousha could not resist his claims during the cold winter nights, and it was easy for him to trick her into lying down with him behind some bushes in the field when all the other workers had left for the day and no one could hear his lusty demands.

Black Ammousha lived in harmony with my light-brown mother. They were like adopted sisters, united by the same culture, the same traditions, and even the same prohibitions. They differed only in color and temperament.

Ammousha enjoyed long conversations, which my mother could not tolerate, thinking that idle babble would lead to sin; therefore, she constantly called on God to forgive her. Ammousha loved to listen to songs and would sway to music when she heard it coming from my room. Unlike Ammousha, my mother warned me whenever she caught me listening to the singer Mohammed Abdu. "Remember," she said, "God will melt iron in the ears of those who listen to songs."

When King Faisal abolished slavery in the 1960s, Ammousha realized that a new era had dawned, one very different from that of her parents. Her father, Jawhar, rushed with his wife, Nweyyir, whose eyes had been blinded and her face marked by smallpox, to see his master, Abdul-Rahman.

"What does this law mean?" he asked.

"You are free as of today," Abdul-Rahman replied, not noticing the terrified look in Jawhar's eyes.

"Where shall we go, Uncle," Jawhar said, "when we know nothing beyond this house and this field?"

My grandfather could not find an answer to the question. He, too, was confused, for slave owners did not know how to function without their slaves. The law, however, was clear: the owner would be compensated for the price of the slave in the event that he was not satisfied with God's rewards and forgiveness. He looked at Nweyyir and her daughter, Ammousha, who was then nine years old.

"You are free today," he said.

Nweyyir turned her back to my grandfather, probing the ground with her cane and muttering words that Ammousha still remembers: "What a crushing freedom! Nothing but cold and hunger."

The winter that year was severe. Jawhar said, "Where do we go, Uncle? Let us work for you, Uncle."

"What will you do? What shall I give you for it?"

"I'm satisfied, Uncle, with the morsels we eat and the small roof over our heads."

It was only when Ammousha's children went to school and wore uniforms just like the children of her "uncles" in the village that she realized they were no longer slaves and she understood my grandfather's words: "You are free."

It took her a long time to comprehend the full meaning of freedom, though she never really relished it but only lived it as a formality. It is difficult to shake off the chains of bondage when other people continue to perpetuate them.

As such she continued to be the small girl who trembled with fear when an uncle or aunt called her name; she would automatically rise to her feet, saying "At your service, Uncle," or "At your service, Aunt." She dared not ignore their demands, even when she was shaking with fever or suffering from postnatal bleeding. She would immediately get out of bed to set the fire in the kiln, make bread, lift a whole lamb out of the cauldron, or cook the food for weddings and banquets. She was content with simple rewards such as clothes for Eid,[6] silver coins, or household delicacies like coffee and cardamom. Later, when big sacks of rice came to the masters from Riyadh, she would be given a pot of grains to prepare in her house for her free children.

Her children fostered friendships with other boys in the village, many of whom were milk brothers, since Ammousha had nursed half of these boys. Had it not been for the color of their skin, Ammousha's children would have sensed no difference between themselves and their peers. However, her daughter Si'da's willful behavior and her son Farraaj's indifference to the orders of the village magnates infuriated those who could not forget that these two had been born into a family of slaves: to them, slavery was not something that could be ended merely by a document issued by the king; slaves would always be slaves. Ammousha did not feel emancipated except through her children, but she did not seem to mind. It sufficed that her children were her link to emancipation.

Many of the village children freely addressed her as "Mother."

---

6. One of two Muslim feasts that celebrate the end of Ramadan, the fasting month, or Hajj, the pilgrimage to Mecca.

Whenever we, the children of the city, went to the village and heard our cousins call her this, we wondered about this black mother whom our relatives always received with so much joy. Women brought her gifts of colorful fabric, silk abayas, or woolen sweaters when they went to visit the village from Riyadh. I once saw her air-kiss my uncle as they embraced in greeting. Mother said Ammousha was her milk sister; Ammousha's mother, Nweyyir, had nursed my mother and my uncle Abdullah with her own children.

When Ammousha's son Farraaj moved to Riyadh to work as the chief of staff in the home of one of the sheikhs, he urged his mother to join him, but she refused. He could not convince her to live with him until the doctors at the village dispensary told her that the illness she had could not be cured except in Riyadh.

Her son's home in Riyadh's Skeriena neighborhood, where she knew hardly anyone, became like a prison to her and aggravated her condition. When Ammousha came to console my mother on the occasion of my father's death, she slept next to her in her bedroom throughout the period of mourning. Mother asked her to stay with us, so she did, becoming her close companion and never leaving her side. Together they went to the neighborhood mosque to pray *taraweeh*, the nightly prayers during Ramadan; to the clinic to check their blood sugar levels and blood pressure, which troubled both of them; to the weddings held by my mother's relatives; and to midmorning gatherings with the women of the neighborhood.

Ammousha was a reservoir of my family's narratives, including their secret stories. Without her, I would not have known much about my own people. My mother grew quieter with age, having exhausted her voice yelling at us in our youth. She would hardly open her mouth except to denounce the younger generation living in what she felt were strange times, or to pray for God's forgiveness. To us, she seemed as harsh as cut stone. I once complained to Ammousha about how cruel Mother was, about how cold she was toward my feelings of sorrow and helplessness, but she dismissed what I said and tried to pacify me.

"Don't blame your poor mother," she consoled.

"Poor mother? Are you serious?" I protested.

"Poor" is the last word one would use to describe my domineering mother. She has never exposed a moment of weakness or complained about poor health. I have never seen her cling to a worldly object or express sorrow for losing it. Nor have I heard her complain of deprivation. I said to Ammousha, "Poor? My mother? Didn't you see how she used to push us away when we showed her love or sympathy? Don't you see how she favors my brothers with gentle treatment while she clamps down on us helpless girls? My mother hates us—because we are girls."

Ammousha repeated her earlier words, her eyes roaming to a distant past. "Don't blame her, my daughter; life was hard on her, and made her hard. Still, she is to be pitied."

Personally, I disagreed. I felt that my mother was a tyrant, not someone to be sorry for. I had never seen her cry, and even when my father died, she made sure to hide her tears from her own children. Some people thought she did not want to upset us with her tears, but we knew that she meant to teach us, as was her custom, a lesson in "resignation during hardships"—patience being the trait of a real Muslim.

Nevertheless, my mother is clever, something that I knew very well. As a child, I thought she had magical powers that revealed to her everything we did. She could detect all our lies and unveil the things we tried to hide. Mother never went to school, but sometimes she did my homework when I started primary school. Checking my schoolbag in the evening, she could tell if I had not answered the reading questions. She would then pull my hair, open my notebook, and push my small head toward the page. "Write!" she would say.

I would lie down on the floor next to the wall in the living room, which served as a dining area during the day and a place to sleep at night, one sheet beneath me and another on top. The men's sitting room was kept closed, clean, and tidy—to be used only for guests.

With my head resting on my small arm, I would start to write, tracing the black dotted letters, which looked like a very long, hard road; the whole night would not be enough to finish them. As I wrote the first line of the letter "ب," sleep would throw sand into my eyes, and I would know that the dot resting under the letter had gotten lost. I would draw just the plate and leave the dot until morning.

Sleeping with the pen in my hand and the notebook for my pillow would be what I recalled of childhood slumber, a dreamlike image, with Mother's figure asking God to end my life and calling me a leprous dog for sleeping without doing my homework.

My joy was always great the following morning when I opened my notebook in class and found that my homework had been done. I thought that my mother, despite the pinch marks she had left on my thighs the night before, was the nicest person in the world. My mother, the magician, who had never gone to school, had done my work.

Oh, my fabulous mother! How much I love you!

As a young girl, I believed everything my mother said—for she knew so much—even when she told us things like how wearing short skirts or bras was haram.[7] To prove it, she would relate the story of a man whose daughter had died. He had buried her, but later realized that he had dropped his car keys in her grave while laying her in the ground, so he retraced his steps to get them. When he opened her grave, he saw flames licking her chest right where her bra had been. Everyone knew that this was her punishment for wearing a bra.

When we were young we didn't see the incongruities in our mother's stories. We thought that she told them to us to entertain, not to scare us. But how could the father bring himself to open the grave? Our imaginations, blinded with fear, clung to the moral of the story, lest we should become that girl, tortured by flames as she entered her grave for wearing a bra in life.

My mother herself never wore a bra. Nor did she use zippers on her clothing—yet another sin about which she wove another story; this time about a young woman who caught fire just along the sweep of the zipper down her back.

Mother used these stories, which other people also knew, to warn us about God's punishment, especially hellfire. She insisted that the flames of this world were nothing but tiny sparks of the colossal fire of hell, where God would melt our skin thousands of times, each time replacing the melted skin with a whole new one.

In my mind, God assumed my mother's face, always angry, always

---

7. Sinful.

threatening; the fire he promised was, on the whole, not much different from the pinches that her fingers burned on the insides of our tender thighs.

I still remember her stories, which dug dreadful furrows in my heart. They pass through my mind, sending shivers down my spine as though I were still a child. I recall the story about a young girl who was kidnapped and subjected to "indecent acts" before she was killed (my mother and Ammousha euphemized rape by using phrases such as "doing it to her" or "breaking her back"). The story, however, does not end there. Before her death, the girl asked her kidnappers to let her go to the bathroom to relieve herself. There she wrote a note to her family in which she disclosed the names and descriptions of her abductors. She slipped the note inside one of the white socks she had worn to school that day.

The police found her dead in the desert, but when her small, innocent body was being washed for burial, the note was discovered and the kidnappers were punished. Thus the story ended with justice bringing death to the wicked. Yet my young mind also understood that the girl was expected to bear the responsibility of being clever and alert; her role must go beyond being the young victim of abduction and rape and murder. Before her death, the girl had to expose her victimizers to prove her innocence and punish the crime. I trembled at night and wet my bed when I recalled the story of the girl with the white socks. I also tried as best I could to remember my duty if I myself got kidnapped: not to die without exposing the wicked men. But the fear inside me focused on another issue, something beyond how to protect myself from being kidnapped: What if they stole me in the afternoon, when I didn't usually wear socks?

In the same way, the story of "The Slippery Black Thief," which later replaced "The Girl with the White Socks," endlessly rattled my sleep even though it sounded like just a series of anecdotes that women exchanged and laughed about when they came to visit my mother in the afternoon. This naked and greasy thief kept hopping from house to house in an area far from our homes, where no one could witness his presence or vouch that the story was real.

My mother's friends joked about him, amusing themselves with different accounts of his numerous adventures. He became popular, like a

TV star, breaking into people's homes on a daily basis, his nimble, naked, slippery body bouncing and gleaming in the dark. Those who chased him had a hard time catching him, and when they did, his oiled limbs slipped out of their hands. I wondered why the women laughed so much as they talked about him. Perhaps the image of a naked black man with dancing genitals tickled them. They would keep their voices down when they referred to his private parts, which they didn't openly name, for sexual organs were either "a man's belongings" or "a woman's belongings."

Despite the suggestive gestures and lewd remarks our neighbor Noura would occasionally make, bashfulness was something the women highly esteemed or even took too far, as in the case of Lateefa, who had moved to the neighborhood from a village east of Riyadh. Lateefa demurely refused to refer to her husband by his name, instead referring to him as "he"—"he went" and "he came back." When the women wanted to know who was going to and fro, she would say, "He!"—astonished that they should ask.

"Who is this 'he'?" they would ask her again.

"He," she'd say, weary of their efforts to push her.

With time, however, Lateefa grew tired of the women's jesting about her shyness and naiveté and became more accustomed to the city's permissive ways and its women's daring discourse. She allowed herself some audacity after bearing her husband five children. He became "our father" instead of "he." The neighbors, however, never heard her mention his name.

In school I learned different stories, sweeter than "The Girl with the White Socks" or "The Slippery Black Thief." Those I read in school didn't cause the rush of fear that the neighborhood stories provoked in me. *Cinderella*, the first one, caught my eye in a colorful book held in the hands of a schoolmate during lunchtime. She read the story as she ate her sandwich, with concentration and joy, as though she were reading it for the first rather than the tenth time. I moved closer, putting my head next to hers, and began to read with equal intensity and pleasure.

The bell rang before I finished reading, rending my heart in two. I was so caught up in the story I forgot where I was; for the first time I knew the cruelty of having to let go of a story only halfway through. My heart pounding with hope and fear and longing, I asked the friend if I could keep the book till I knew how it ended.

"Can I take it home with me? Please? I'll give you whatever you want."
I hugged the book to my breast, my face pleading.

"Sure," she said, rather indifferently. "Then give me one of yours. If you lend to me, I'll lend to you." She had in mind a book-exchange program.

"Agreed," I said.

I had to lie. Besides my schoolbooks, I didn't have a single piece of paper at home. When my mother looked for something on which to write the number of a friend, she would tear a piece of paper out of our old notebooks, some of which she kept for their unused pages. I had to borrow a storybook from Jawhara to lend to Nawal, with the promise that I would lend *Cinderella* to Jawhara when I finished reading it.

I saw myself as Cinderella—orphaned, motherless. Her stepmother was my mother, who constantly beat me and made me do household chores. I, too, wanted to escape a house where no one loved me. When I discovered that a young prince took Cinderella away from her misery, I decided to search for a prince of my own. I found him in our handsome neighbor, Salem, who was ten years older than me and the only young man I knew who was the right age to be the prince. My heart throbbed every time Salem passed by our house, where I stood watching the street. He would look at me and smile as I extended one of my feet, sometimes wearing a shoe, sometimes not, for he was the one who would one day slip the golden shoe onto it. My love for Salem continued to fuel my childish fantasies until the day I came to hate him.

On that day Salem was walking home around two in the afternoon, and as usual I had been waiting for him while playing near our door. He turned his head right and left, and when he saw no one around he blew me a kiss. I leapt in fear, and shouted as I ran away, "Animal!"

The following week I found that Jawhara had another story, *Layla of the Red Dress*. I wonder whether it was my newfound love for reading that kept searching for stories or whether it was sheer fate that tossed them my way and ferried me to unfamiliar lands. In this case, perhaps it was Layla's mother, who constantly warned her clean, fair-skinned, gentle daughter about the wicked wolf. Layla would always listen to her mother and heed her warnings, and though the wolf kept hounding her, stalking her, and charging at her, he was never able to hurt her. She escaped his molestations because she was a well-mannered, obedient girl.

Layla's safety brought me some peace every time I read her story. I would breathe a sigh of relief and say to myself, "Thank God she's safe, thank God! Imagine what would've happened to *me* if the wolf had eaten her!" And I asked God to destroy the evil wolf.

Layla's safety and Cinderella's marriage were happy events in my life. They comforted me and made me stop wetting my bed at night. Before I went to sleep, I imagined myself as Layla, wearing my beautiful red dress and skipping and singing through our neighborhood, which looked like the woods in the story. I was confident that Layla would not die like the girl with the white socks in my mother's story. Cinderella would be rescued by a handsome prince on a white horse; she wouldn't face the terror of falling into the hands of thieves, like the black and oily one, whom I saw in every man on the street. Danger became a wolf living in a faraway forest, present only in pictures. I loved stories that turned danger into a thrill, straining my nerves, following me, threatening me . . . My father would come to kill the wolf; I'd rush to the safety of my mother's arms. My body would relax, rolling in pleasure, as though my imaginings had actually happened.

These stories fed my mind on a world without which I could not have been creative in later years: a world more tranquil, more convivial than our own, a comfortable world in which mothers did not scream at or hit their daughters; in which girls could play with boys without the fear of being punished or threatened with death; in which I loved a handsome young man who wouldn't violate my sense of decency by blowing me a kiss, but who would smile at me and stroke my hair with love and tenderness. I spent a lot of time daydreaming about this world. Sometimes I couldn't make up my mind: Should I be the small girl playing and amusing herself, like Layla of the red dress, or should I be the beautiful young woman, like Cinderella, who is in love with a young man and dances with him? Which young man should I love: the handsome singer Khalid al-Sheikh, who was on TV, or Hatim Ali, the Syrian actor? Or should I go for Nawal's neighbor, who was closer to my age? Daydreaming was easy to do, so I created a comfortable space in which I gathered all those I loved in a single scene and gave each a different role.

For a period of time Khalid al-Sheikh managed to fill a big space in these dreams. I loved him. I adored him. I saw his image everywhere

I went. Swept up in my imaginings, I would forget all about the world around me. Until one day my mother caught me while I pretended to rock in Khalid's lap, hugging my pillow and clutching the bottom of it between my thighs. With my arms wrapped around it, I could feel the heat of my breath leaving my mouth and moving to my cheek, then to my neck. I held on to his lap—the pillow between my thighs—till he suddenly fell to the floor and raised a foot to kick me in the face. I opened my eyes to see that my mother had pulled the pillow out from between my thighs and was smacking me with it. From then on I stopped meeting Khalid al-Sheikh in the living room, where Mother could watch, and started to see him on the terrace where I slept away from her sleeping area, for she watched even my daydreams and punished me for them.

I was transformed by the stories that I read. I stopped being the reckless child who lived for play and turned into a sensitive and emotional girl, dreamy-eyed, easily provoked, easily dejected. I would leave my games to muse on things. Looking at the sky, I would see Cinderella's carriage, the horses that pull it, the lions in the jungle, all the trees growing there, and the hair of the prince falling down to his shoulders. I also turned the radio on to hear songs that made me think of my love for the singers Khalid al-Sheikh and Abdul-Majeed Abdullah.

New needs surfaced inside me that had not been urgent before. Watered by rampant desires, the seeds that stories planted in my chest grew into tall trees in a boundless forest. It cleaved my heart to see those trees turn into mirages as I came closer to them, as I ran and panted for them. They tortured me, floating with their thorny tops on the surface of my heart. I wanted my mother to throw her arms around me when I came home from school, tired and full of fears as if I had been chased by a wolf. I wanted her to place her hand on my head, to give me cold water to drink, to ward off my fears and calm my heart while invoking the Lord's name, as she would do when my brother Fahad was sick.

She beat me instead, every time I came home, on account of being late—always late. I got easily distracted by the sight of boys playing games with picture cards or splashing each other with frothing Pepsi bottles. In time, however, my mind arrived at an equation, a just equation, which I followed throughout the years I was allowed to play on the street. I made sure that my hours of play were equal in weight to the blows I received from my mother. It was sad to see other girls going home so early. I thought that the beating I would get for one hour of play, which passed so quickly, was not fair at all; therefore, I aimlessly roamed the nearby alleys looking for more fun to make up for the punishment I would get when I went home.

In the time and place where I grew up, mothers did not usually worry when their sons were away from the house, nor did they insist on their coming home early. On these grounds I built my relationships with the boys on the street, eventually becoming their friend. Only boys could enjoy playing games as much as I did after school. I joined their games of picture cards, which had images of movie stars we hardly knew at the time, such as Elvis Presley and Clint Eastwood, the actor in cowboy films. I also jumped on the tires with the boys, my dress slipping up to show my legs every time I hopped from one tire to another. Then I started riding behind them on their bikes. This was the sight that almost killed my mother when she saw me. She couldn't wait to tell my father.

"She's gone too far! Riding behind S'eidan and holding on to his waist!"

My father neither responded nor showed concern. So she yelled at him to wake him up from his stupor, or rather to plant terror in his heart—the way one character in an evening TV show yelled at her husband in her Upper Egyptian dialect and drove him to kill his own daughter: "Your daughter is pregnant, Hreidy!"

My mother was aiming to shake my father out of his permissiveness. "Your daughter is playing with boys, Othman!" she said.

My father saw nothing more than innocent play in my spending time with boys, but my mother pulled my hair till she tore a clump of it out. After planting five blue pinch marks on my thigh, she said to me, "I'll kill you if I see you playing with boys again!"

Mother would surely have killed me had she known how the adults dealt with me. As I ran around in the sun, looking for some pleasure that would offset the physical pain and blue marks on my thighs, I sometimes found myself alone. Adult men, too, found me alone and took advantage of the situation to press their organs against my small body or thrust their hands inside my panties, in return for some sweets or a coin for a chocolate bar. I grew up hating chocolate without exactly knowing why, yet I didn't hate the men who molested me. One of them was a relative; I thought he couldn't possibly want to hurt me.

The romantic girl I had become as a result of my reading drove me to search for mothers in school. I liked to imagine Mother as an elegant, smiling young woman who wore a bra, a skirt, and stylish sandals—just like my schoolteacher Miss Fatima, who we girls imagined had come from a faraway magic island. She was fair, with a face made more attractive by light makeup of kohl and pink lipstick. She also wore high heels. I projected her image on my mother and went around singing: "Mother, Mother, how charming you are!"

Feelings for teacher and mother became intertwined. I copied my teacher's clothes and pasted them on the figure of my mother. Their features blended; I hardly knew Fatima from Heila. I liked them the same. But it didn't take long to discover that both had the same temperament. One day Fatima slapped me on the face, then made me stand by the wall on one foot, because I hadn't memorized the table for counting by six. Fatima and Heila were one and the same in reality, not just in my dreams.

On the way home, I still sang my song about mothers: "Mother, Mother, how charming you are!" I wanted her to hear the song I'd learned at school. So I threw my bag down near the door and ran to her. She was standing at the stove browning onions for the midday meal, my young brother crying near her legs. She pushed him with her foot.

"Go away! Move away from the fire! May Allah end your life!"

His crying, I thought, was going to spoil the magic of the moment.

"Why is he crying?" I asked her in a tone full of blame for my brother.

"He's hungry and I have no time to nurse him. Take him away from me!"

"Mother, I have a song for you."

"What? You sing? Blasted girl! Take your brother away from me."

"I mean a chant," I said. "A memorization lesson."

"Take your brother away! May Allah never remember you!"

I hated my brother Ibrahim; he spoiled my song and my mother's mood, not that her mood wasn't always spoiled. I carried him screaming on my hip, his legs around my waist, and rocked him a little. He continued to cry.

"Listen, listen," I said. "Mother, listen to me."
Before she could respond, I went on to sing:

Mother, Mother, how charming you are.
Always in my heart, how precious you are.

"Waaaaaaa," Ibrahim continued to cry.
"Hush, hush." I rocked him twice on my hip to get him to stop, but he wouldn't. Even in childhood, Ibrahim was troublesome and hateful! He spoiled all the songs of my life.
"Stop crying," I said to him, resuming my song:

Always in my heart, I'll never forget you.
May your life be very long, Mother!

I finished my song, but the moment was not tender, the way I wanted it to be. Still, I hoped my mother would throw her arms around me after she had heard the song; I even thought of putting the baby down so that she could hug me properly, with body and soul. Instead she took the big spoon out of the pot and brought it to my face. "Get out of my way before I whack you on the head with this spoon!"
My mind had learned to deny such events to protect me from pain. Later it did the same thing with all that was unromantic in my life by projecting the opposite image. On this occasion, it told me that Mother was not at all angry with me or my song; she was angry with Ibrahim and his silly crying. For she also said, "May Allah not let you live one more day. Your brother has shattered my head with his screaming!"

Two

ONE AFTERNOON, we were playing near the house with the children of relatives who had come to visit and would stay with us till the evening. Mother sliced a watermelon for the guests, filling the house with its sweet smell. That evening, she would burn some incense and pass it around the visitors herself before they left. The two smells were linked in my mind with guests, happiness, and freedom without punishment. Too busy with her guests, Mother would forget about us. The house would be calm and free from yelling, and we ourselves would have our liberty till the guests went away.

Facing the door, my relative Noura covered her eyes with her hands and counted to ten. My sister Mashael and I ran to hide behind a neighbor's car right across from our house.

Breathing rapidly, I shut my eyes, excited by the game and afraid that Noura would find my hiding place. A heavy hand descended on me, reaching for my breast from behind the tire. Something cracked in my chest, like a sob, which I can't quite explain. Without thinking, I ran home. Noura's words followed me. "You left the game! You lose!"

I passed by the sitting room, where my mother's guests were still talking and laughing. The door to our storage room was open, so it was dimly lit near the entrance. I wanted to hide, not to be seen by the guests, a need as urgent as being desperate to pee. The walls around my chest suddenly crumbled and salty fluid stung my eyes. I was just about to cry when I saw the sack of rice, standing straight at half my height. I rested my face on the sack, put my arms around it, and gave in to weeping.

My chest felt lighter and my breathing easier, freer, and cleaner. I had some peace. From then on, every time the giant extended a hand to grab my chest, I would hurry to the sack of rice, which was always ready to hold me as I cried. Then I would go back to playing, not wanting to miss any games.

The giant continued to follow me, especially after the evening when our bachelor neighbor, Mohammed, called me in and shut the door and wouldn't free me until I cried for a long time. I woke up that night choked by tears. Mother heard me while she prayed.

"What's wrong with you?" she asked.

"A tall giant! I can only see his big feet. He sits on my chest and suffocates me."

"This is Jathoom,"[8] she said. "You must have slept without mentioning Allah's name. Say bismillah;[9] then read al-mu'awwidhat[10] before you sleep."

"I said bismillah; I read all three Qur'anic suras. It didn't work."

Jathoom continued to suffocate me, his visits coming closer and closer together. He arrived when the sun had trailed its orange gown away from our door and wrapped it around the neck of the sky. The giant would come wearing the black mantle of the night, which he spread over the place just so that no one could see him suffocate me and muffle my voice. I had to switch on the lights when I went to sleep.

Once my breasts started to grow into two little buds, I couldn't play outside anymore. I sat alone in our small yard while my siblings scattered around the neighborhood. At that time, it made me happy to be older, indifferent to games. I managed to buy a tape recorder, which a younger cousin sold me at a profit for ten riyals. Certain that my mother would

---

8. In Arabic myth, "Jathoom" (incubus) refers to a jinni or an evil spirit that takes the form of a lover and copulates with sleeping women. In this context, however, the mother has in mind the evil jinni that appears after sunset to torture human beings, male or female, by sitting on their chests and causing shortness of breath and an accelerated heartbeat. Mentioning Allah's names and reading verses from the Qur'an before sleeping are believed to keep the Jathoom away.

9. In the name of Allah.

10. According to Muslims, reading the three short suras (a group of verses) from the Qur'an called al-mu'awwidhat al-thalatha (the three suras that ward off evil) can protect humans from all kinds of unpleasant events and creatures.

not buy it for me, I stole the money from the pocket of my father's *thobe*,[11] which he had hung in the living room before he went to do his ablutions for the *'asr* prayer.[12] All I wanted was a tape recorder of my own, to hang on my shoulder while I wander around listening to the songs of Abdul Haleem, Umm Kulthoum, and Warda al-Jazairiyya.[13] I would live through their passionate loves, longing for a lost lover.

I also discovered that writing about how I felt was easy and safe. In writing I found a different world, one I shared with a host of people whom I chose all by myself, people I loved and who loved me back. Writing gave me a cool, fortified cave, where no one but me could enter or discover the secret. The cave was sealed with a private code that I alone could decipher, for neither of my parents could read well.

For the first time, I found a hiding place away from the neighborhood alleys and their rough men. Away, too, from daydreams. I grew tired of changing the faces in their scenes; I also fought with Khalid al-Sheikh, who traveled to finish his studies and left me behind because I felt the urge to cry. I had to send him far away from my daydreams to cry over him, but I didn't bring him back because my tears helped me more than he did.

---

11. This is the traditional white garment worn by men in some parts of the Arab world, especially the Gulf region and Saudi Arabia.
12. Midafternoon prayer, one of the five daily prayers prescribed for Muslims.
13. Three famous Egyptian singers.

Three

MY MOTHER COULD NOT read well, but she could piece together the letters of the alphabet and understand simple sentences, such as "Omar went to the baker." However, she did not comprehend statements like "You are embers slumbering in my heart, aroused by songs," or "a rose I water every night with your love." Nevertheless, her reading skills got me in trouble one day when she found, while inspecting the contents of my bag, a piece of paper on which I had written "Ghazi Algoseibi, *Shiqqat al-hurriyya*."[14] She faced me with it, putting one hand on her waist and shaking the other, as though she had caught me with blood on my hands.

"May Allah disgrace you! Who is this Ghazi, you shameless girl? And what is this 'apartment'?"

I trembled. My heart drummed like an electric engine dashing forward, almost flying out of terror, although I did not plan to meet anyone in any apartment. She shoved the paper in my face, and I realized what she meant. Smiling, I told her, "Ghazi Algoseibi is the name of a writer. *Shiqqat al-hurriyya* is the title of his book."

"Aha! You lie, too."

"I swear to Allah I'm not lying. Ask anyone, they'll tell you."

"And you swear by Allah's name! It is Allah who exposed you, blasted girl."

---

14. This novel, written by the Saudi author Ghazi Algoseibi (1940–2010), has been translated into English by Leslie McLoughlin as *An Apartment Named Freedom* (Kegan-Paul, 1996). During his life Algoseibi held several political posts and was known for his liberal ideas.

I didn't look disturbed, as I usually did whenever I was in trouble. Nor did I chew on my lip or stammer or have a dry mouth. I just laughed. She felt trapped. Still, she took the piece of paper to show my brother Fahad. She didn't return from his room to tell me that my case was hopeless and that, as usual, Allah had intervened to disgrace me.

On these occasions Mother would speak on Allah's behalf. If she happened to discover that I had gone against her beliefs, she assured me that it was Allah, not she, who had caught me in the act.

"The Lord has laughed!" she would say, following the statement with one of the Prophet's sayings, which she rendered in the colloquial expression "When Allah's messenger, peace be upon him, was one day asked, 'Messenger of the Lord, what do you call a *hidden* thing?,' his answer was 'the thing which shouldn't have been done.'"

God, as my mother portrayed him, continued to chase me for a long time, disturbing my peace and terrifying me. If I tasted a moment of pleasure, I couldn't help feeling that God, being cruel like my mother, would go tell on me and send her to wreck the happiness I had, even if I were thousands of miles away from her.

In my prayers I would try to envision God's image as I read verses from the Qur'an, to humble my heart and give it some peace; but all I could see was Mother's face, her kohl-lined eyes, reddish and half-closed, ridden with trachoma. I would shudder. For a long time, I carried with me this image of God, who resembled Mother in his cruelty.

Following the event of *Shiqqat al-hurriyya*, my mother felt quite defeated, having discovered her illiteracy; a few days later, she decided to attend a school for adult education.

On the first day of classes, she came home just before the *maghrib* prayer[15] carrying books, notebooks, and a pencil. To match her joy my father said: "*Masha Allah!*[16] Where were you? Shopping?"

"No, at school," she proudly said, like a diligent schoolgirl.

We, her daughters, had a new responsibility added to our household

---

15. The fourth daily prayer in Islam, which takes place at *maghrib* (sunset).
16. Literally, this expression means "whatever Allah wills." It is often used to express goodwill and ward off the evil eye when commenting on a person's wealth or success, among other things.

chores: helping Mother with her homework. It gave her pleasure to show us that she, too, was going to school.

She regularly went to the literacy school, which held its classes in the afternoon. The question that tickled my mind focused on the motives that took her to school. Was she ashamed of her ignorance? Or did she want to upgrade the skills she used to detect her daughters' disobedience?

Four

WHEN I DISCOVERED that I was pregnant, my husband was exceedingly happy. He insisted that we go to the clinic that very day to make sure the home test was correct. Two hours later the clinic test came out positive.

"Does the blood test show the gender of the fetus?" he asked the doctor.

"It's too early, my dear," she said in Egyptian Arabic. "Gender will show up in the fourth month, sometimes in the fifth. I know you men are very eager to have sons. May Allah grant you your desire. A boy is sweet in his father's eyes, but do pray, too, for your wife's safe delivery."

"Amen."

The results of a test in the fourth month were not to Mansur's satisfaction. The doctor was embarrassed when she saw his face darken with vexation.

"It appears to be a girl, the little rascal," the doctor said, running the instrument over my belly. "It's a girl, sweet little thing."

"Please make sure, Doctor!" Mansur said.

The doctor looked at my face, which had started to show distress, not because of the sex of the fetus but because of Mansur's reaction: he couldn't control his emotions even in front of the doctor.

"You know, Mr. Mansur," the doctor said, "sometimes the ultrasound may show the fetus as a girl, but in the end a boy comes out."

Mansur's face lit up with relief, as if he had already been granted a boy. "Is that right?" he said.

"I bet you anything!" the doctor said. "I've seen many people who had this happen to them. You just pray to God for a boy! It's all in the hands of the Lord, the Almighty, the ultimate giver."

Mansur continued to dream about having a boy. "I'll call him Saʿad, after my father."

"It's most probably a girl," I said.

"I told you it's a boy, and I'll call him Saʿad. Did you hear me? I don't want to hear any more."

My mother said, not because she loved girls but because she pitied Mansur, "Thanks be to Allah for everything, Mansur. Girls are a merciful gift."

"Thanks be to Allah for everything," Mansur said, as he looked from a distance at my baby after her birth. Then he left my room.

He called that evening from Bahrain to say that he was spending the weekend with his friends, for a change. I didn't see him for a whole week.

On the first day after delivery, I cried now and then, not knowing why. I recalled the tunnel of hell I had passed through as I was giving birth, the lashes of pain burning my back.

I am running inside a tunnel when I see a gate with swinging doors, opening and closing. I tell myself, don't fret, this must be the very end. I push the doors to pass through; they howl as they close behind me. I find myself in darkness again, in the same corridor of pain . . . I race through it only to face another gate. Be patient, I say, maybe this is the last gate. But the last one never comes. I wake up terrified, Ammousha's voice, not my mother's, coming to me through the darkness: "*Bismillah al-Rahman al-Rahim!*[17] What's wrong?"

"I had a nightmare, Aunt Ammousha!" But I went on to recount another dream that haunted me even more.

I had dreamed I was lying on my back, nursing my daughter. Then I slept in my dream, and when I woke up, I anxiously looked for her. She was not in her bed. I found her in mine, right under me. I had rolled over and suffocated her. I reached to touch her hand. It felt icy, distinctly so. Gripped with fear I shook her body. It was cold and dead and rubbery, except for one little part, which had continued to be warm, giving me

---

17. In the name of Allah, the most gracious, the most compassionate.

some hope that she might still be alive. I called her, "Hayaat! Hayaat!,"[18] which was not her name, as I surfaced out of my dream.

Ammousha brought me a drink, a yellow infusion in which she had steeped a piece of paper bearing verses from the Qur'an written in saffron. It emitted a calming smell.

"Read al-mu'awwidhat, my daughter, to be protected against Satan. Women in childbed do have nightmares."

I asked myself, as I reflected on my dream, why I had called my daughter Hayaat? Was the dream linked to my infant or to my own cold and dying life with Mansur? Did the baby's warm spot promise some warmth for my life, too? I did not find this analysis too far removed from reality, but which part of my life still pulsed, signifying hope? Was this infant the only hope left in it? I looked at the baby, whose father had not come back to give her a name; he wouldn't care, since she wasn't born a boy. Should I call her Amal?[19]

I felt that the baby was a burden to me. Whenever I turned to look at her, my heart grew heavy with tears. Had she come to disturb my life? Every part of my being hurt: the raw wound between my thighs, my breasts swollen with milk. The baby cried all night, constantly wet with urine and feces, and slept all day. Then there was my mother, resigned to Allah's judgment and will—for He is the One who grants girls—and Mansur, who escaped to Bahrain to deal with his shock. He called me, drunk, with tears in his voice. "How is the little one?" And he drunkenly added when he heard her crying, "Why couldn't she be a boy? I would've loved the two of you so much more, and brought you here to be with me. Screw you women!"

Mansur left home to drink and forget about his disappointment in his firstborn's sex. He allowed himself the freedom to do anything and everything because God had not fulfilled his grand dream to be "Abu Sa'ad."[20]

Ammousha sat with me and administered all the traditional childbed remedies: black seeds for general wellbeing, myrrh solutions to disinfect

---

18. Given to girls in the Arab and Islamic world, the name Hayaat literally means "life."
19. Another Arabic name for girls, meaning "hope."
20. Literally, "the father of Sa'ad."

the wound, fenugreek to increase the milk, and anise seeds for gas. But the stories she told me were the medicine my soul needed.

She looked into the baby's eyes and said, "Don't be sad, my daughter. How could anyone feel sad when they have this little beauty?"

She picked up the baby and played with her as with a doll. She made her smile by putting her finger on the baby's lips and gently patting them. "This girl will take care of you when you are old like me," Ammousha said. "She will be the joy of your home. She will pour coffee for her father, and he will love her more than all his other children."

"That seems unlikely, Ammousha. The man has already run away."

"This is what you see now, my dear girl. I'll be reminding you in the future. They say that the birth of a son is joyful at first, but in the end, the girl will be the blessed child, like the dutiful Mae, who was more devoted to her father than any one of his sons."

"What is the story of this Mae?"

Mae was the daughter of a blind and elderly man, Ammousha told me. Many young men wanted to marry her, but she refused, saying that her father needed her. She feared that any future husband would make it hard for her to care for her father. One day, an eligible man proposed to her. Her father didn't have the heart to turn him away.

"I would want you to have a son," he said to her. "A son will come to your aid, Mae. I won't always be here for you."

Mae got married and had children, boys and girls. One day the tribe decided to move to new pastures after a drought had dried up their land and killed their crops. But because Mae's father was too weak to travel, the tribe decided to leave him behind with some food placed next to him. Mae had to leave with the clan, against her will. After traveling for a long and tiring day, the caravan stopped to eat and rest. They built a fire, and everyone wanted to enjoy talking over a longed-for cup of coffee.

Mae's husband asked her to bring him their infant son to play with him.

"I left him in my father's care," Mae calmly said.

"You must be joking," he said, terrified. "Say it's not so!"

"I have nothing else to say."

"How could you leave my son with your father in the wilderness? Have you gone mad?"

"Your son is no more precious to me than my father," Mae responded. "As you anguish for your son, so do I for my father."

Rising to his feet, he mounted his horse and galloped away, tearing through the pitch-black night hoping to find his son alive and not eaten by wolves. He flew through the wilderness, fear constantly ripping his heart, which had learned a lesson in love. As he neared the spot where the clan had left Mae's blind father, a loud voice rang in his ears. "Go away!" the voice warned. "This is Mae's son!"

Mae's father was guarding her son by using his cane to beat the ground every time he heard the rustling of trees or the noises of insects. "Move away from Mae's son," he would cry.

Mae's husband picked up his son and his wife's father, like two small children, and returned with them to his clan. The story became known to people as a witness to and an example of the tenderness and loyalty that a daughter has for her father. It is even believed that the man whom God has not blessed with a daughter could not possibly know the true taste of kindness.

I slept that night with my heart warmly wrapped by Mae's story, happy with the justice of heaven, which creates female children not to harm them but to be proud of their faithfulness. To honor my daughter, I decided to call her Mae.

Five

MOTHER'S INTELLIGENCE and magic powers continued to surprise me. "How is it you can count and do addition when you never went to school?" I asked her one day.

This praise inspired her to tell me her story, which she related with the pride of an army general revealing one of his secret tactics. "I used to overhear my brother Abdullah and my half-brother Mohammed while they read their lessons in the sitting room of our village house. I listened in on what they said and learned it, too. I got to know the numbers and letters and some sentences. One day, however, Mohammed caught me using charcoal to write with a smart hand on his wooden board. He pulled my braid, almost tearing it off, and threw me out of the room. 'If I see you here again, I'll break your leg!' he said.

"In the village it came to be known that Heila could count to one thousand, so the boys hovered around me to test my knowledge. 'Do you really know how to count to one thousand?' I rose to the challenge and started by counting to one hundred, a point at which some of the boys acknowledged that they had lost their bet, while others walked away, resentful that they didn't catch me making mistakes."

"Did you really know how to count to one thousand?" I asked her.

"Yes! What did you think? In fact, when your father, who worked in Riyadh, came to visit our village, he saw me challenging the village boys by counting extra fast. So he asked them, 'Masha Allah, who is this clever girl?' Although I was quite bashful at the time, I still blurted out, 'I am Heila bint Abdul-Muhsin!' I wish Allah had ended my life the day I said it; I wish I hadn't."

"Why, Mother? Didn't he know you? Wasn't he your relative? Wasn't my dad your father's cousin?"

"This . . . yes, on that day your father went to mine to ask for my hand. My father said, 'Come next year. Heila is still very young. She is an orphan and lives with her grandmother, who won't let us take her away to marry her off at the moment.' Every year, for three years, my father continued to tell Othman to come back the following year, till the day I married him. I had just returned from the field when my family picked me up. I didn't know what was happening then, being so young, not having had my period yet. And I would never have guessed that my counting would send me hurtling down an alien road, endlessly long, like the numbers themselves."

My mother fell silent. She seemed absorbed by a vision of what she called her long and alien road.

I asked her to continue, putting my hand on hers to encourage her. She pulled her hand away and said, "Leave me now; you have taken my mind off my prayers. What's the use of all this talk? It can only add to our sins. May Allah forgive us all. You too. Get up and say your prayers."

Ammousha completed my mother's skimpy narrative: Heila, who had not menstruated yet, came back from her herding mission, which was then a chore that young girls usually did. Her father had ordered his sons, Abdullah and Mohammed, and Ammousha's brother S'eidan to slaughter the wedding sheep. He had also commissioned Nweyyir, Ammousha's mother, and Wad-ha, Heila's grandmother (who brought her up after the death of her mother, Selma), to prepare Heila for her wedding to Othman, who was coming from Riyadh that very day to claim his bride. Heila had been hoping to have, before sundown, a meal of bread soaked in a broth of onion and ghee, which her grandmother was cooking for supper, and the smell of bread, freshly baked in the home kiln, was mouthwatering. If she could only have enough time to eat her meal, she told herself. When she stepped into the house, a long hand pulled her dress. "Come here, blasted girl! Why are you so late?"

Heila had not intended to be late, but drowsiness had lengthened her road. Grandma Wad-ha wasn't actually angry with her; she was just feeling tense on that particular night. God knows what kind of destiny it had in store for her young charge.

Nweyyir tightly fastened the strings of the girl's drawers, wrapping them around her waist to protect her. From what, Nweyyir didn't know. That way, she thought, no one could easily untie them.

Before he left for the dawn prayer, the man pulled the sleeping girl to him by her waist, the way she had seen them handle her wedding sheep on her way home from the field. The groom must accomplish his mission before leaving the room on the morning after the wedding; otherwise, people would laugh at him. Without saying a word, he pulled her feet beneath him and mounted her, stopping her kicks with his thighs. He stabbed his knife into the tender flesh between her legs and left her bleeding, as if it was a normal thing to do. Heila was terrified. She thought her father would kill her if she told him about what his cousin had done. How could she tell him about something so embarrassing? How could she utter the shameful words to explain what had happened? Her mind told her, as she thought of the words her grandmother and Nweyyir had spoken to her, that they had tried to prepare her for this; but she didn't quite understand. Every one of their words meant that she should submit, like all good women, to what Othman would do to her, even if she didn't like it. This meant that they would all forgive him, no matter what he did to her. But she herself would never forgive him or accept what he did. She couldn't possibly love this man who had terrorized her on that night; she continued to harbor these feelings toward him throughout her life.

Something that felt like fear turned her stomach and pressed hard on her ribcage on that first night with him, but on subsequent nights it turned into a feeling of disgust followed by severe nausea. And yet her mind continued to insist that she listen to all the proclamations that urge a woman to be patient and responsive in bed and warn her against Allah's punishment if she refuses her husband's demands. She should endure the sexual act till he's finished, consoling herself with being rewarded in paradise.

Heila ran away twice after her wedding night. She took off first to her maternal uncle's nearby village, walking almost half a day to reach his house, hardly thinking of bandits or thieves. Helpless and exhausted, she threw herself on her uncle Dari's shoulder.

Her uncle seemed unconcerned by her complaints. He asked God to bless her mother's soul and patted her head with his hand, saying, "If your mother had been here, you wouldn't have run away." He took her hand and walked back with her to her own village. Both were silent until they came to her family's house. She saw her own brothers playing near the door as though nothing had ever happened. But when Wad-ha saw Heila, she beat her hard and pinched her thighs, leaving marks that lasted many days. The girl might have died from the beating she received that night, had it not been for Nweyyir's intervention.

On the following day, no one could find her. She had disappeared once again. Her brother Abdullah did not find her at her uncle's, where he was sent to look for her. The family beat her half-sister, Sarah, to make her tell them where Heila had gone, but Sarah, worried about her sister, cried for a long time and swore that she knew nothing.

"Maybe a jinni kidnapped Heila and broke her neck near the well," Sarah said to her grandmother.

"I wish he had kidnapped you, too, to spare us any more shame, you blasted girl," Sarah's mother said.

Night came and still no trace of Heila. Her family started to be truly worried, but Nweyyir had some soothing words for Wad-ha.

"Don't worry! Heila is still young; she won't go far. She'll come back when the sun fills the house tomorrow morning. Where could she go? She must be here or there. She'll be back."

"The girl is young," Wad-ha said. "She may have fallen into a well or something we don't know yet."

Exhausted after staying up late that night, Nweyyir said goodbye to Wad-ha and went to sleep in her own house. She walked the short distance between Wad-ha's house and her own, crickets around her breaking the silence of the night as though leading her to Heila's hiding place or keeping her company by having a raucous party full of cryptic night sounds. Nweyyir went into her house, which consisted of a small kitchen and a smaller bedroom, the gift of her "uncle" Abdul-Rahman. It was empty of her children: Ammousha had already been married, and her sons had left home to work with Aramco in Khobar.

In the narrow corridor she stood near the earthenware jar to have some water. She had removed the wooden lid and taken a draught to wet her mouth—dry on account of her fear for Heila—when her foot bumped into a small, warm object.

"*Bismillah al-Rahman al-Rahim!* Are you human or jinn?"

A voice sounded, shaking with sobs as well as fear. "It's me, Grandma Nweyyir. Heila."

Nweyyir walked with Heila to her grandmother's house, holding the girl's small hand, which was shaking with hunger and cold, and patting her head as she recited tales of hardships, patience, and solace to calm her down.

Heila was not thinking about how her grandmother would punish her, being hungry and tired and helpless after a whole day of running and hiding. She thought of the taste of food in her mouth and found it better than the taste of freedom she had just experienced. "Hunger is godless!" she had once heard her father say.

The two walked home not knowing which one was guiding the other, the blind Nweyyir or the sighted Heila. Both walked the road without eyes; the night had veiled Heila's eyes and put in chains the last day she spent in her village.

She had spent two days hiding from all those who pushed her toward a man fifteen years her senior, a man she dreaded seeing as she recalled the day he had asked her name. She wished she had never told him. Her loose tongue, which her granny had warned her about, must be behind what had happened to her. Without it, none of this would have happened. Talking became abhorrent to her from that day forward. She decided to use speech as sparingly as possible, to guard against sin and disaster, or perhaps to punish herself.

Othman returned to claim his bride the following day. He kept her feet tied all night so that she couldn't flee him again. In the morning he traveled with her to Riyadh, where she knew no roads for escape.

Six

❧

I USED A STRAINER to stop the cardamom husks from falling into the thermos, poured the bitter coffee, and tightened the lid. I threw some dates into a plastic container, which I put, along with the thermos, in a plastic basket. I took it with me to the back seat of the family car, driven by a Filipino man, to go to my work at al-Watan Hospital. The air was cool and Fayruz[21] was singing: "How are you? It's been a while!"

The car raced through the fast ring road, doing over 100 km/h without the heavy traffic Riyadh's streets usually see during rush hours. On the way to the hospital we passed by undeveloped land that used to be, according to my father, desert sought by picnickers in the spring. Now it forms part of the city, only twenty minutes from our house. At the hospital's gate, I put on my burka before the armed guard could glimpse me as he peered in for the parking sticker on the windshield.

Taking a job as a social worker at the hospital was the only option available to me when I left Mansur and returned to my father's house after his death. I wanted to work to support myself and my daughter, and when I found this well-paying job with the American company running the hospital, my mother had no good reason to stop me from working there—though she still complained that the job would entail mixing with men, which would in turn expose me to idle gossip. Besides, she said, my child's father would mock our family and might take the baby from me. My mother knew that Mansur didn't care what I did after his second marriage, but she wanted me to believe my work at the hospital could turn my

---

21. A famous Lebanese singer.

life into a hell. In reality she was worried that the job would save me from her watchful eye and criticism for many hours a day; it would also lead to my independence, and she would no longer be able to control me as she could when I depended on what she gave me out of her pocket.

I promised her that I would wear the burka like all the other Saudi girls from respectable families, and I told her the number of other women who would be working with me in the same department. When she realized she could not win, she opted to be satisfied with my adherence to the burka until she could find another pretext to end my working at the hospital. I wore the burka, which showed nothing but my eyes, although my fellow employees were aware that the face cover would be lifted once we were inside the office. I myself would forget to put it back on my face when a male colleague or patient came to the office.

"Good morning."

"Good morning to Indians,[22] to happiness and broken eggs."[23]

"Good morning, Emily."

"Good morning, Madame Hend."

"Where's the attendance book, care-free girl?"

"With the manager, my darling."

"It seems that we have to face Susu[24] again so early in the morning. Good gracious!"

I headed for the office of Sarah, our manager. The smell of her American coffee, as well as her American perfume, filled the corridor. Sarah graduated from an American university. She doesn't wear the burka when she walks through the lobbies, and she wraps her head with only a black silk scarf that reveals some of her hair in front.

Sarah is divorced and in her forties; she wears cosmetics that make her look even older. What bothers her most is the defiance of male employees under her supervision. They don't listen to her orders simply because she is a woman, and they refuse to go to her office at eight a.m. to sign the

---

22. This is meant to be a humorous reference to Hend's name, which is pronounced like the Arabic word for India (al-Hind). Hunood, the Arabic word used in the text, is the plural of Hindi (Indian).

23. Again, the intention here is to be humorous. In Arabic, the three coordinated expressions rhyme, creating a light, rhythmic way of speaking.

24. A tongue-in-cheek nickname name for Sarah, the manager.

attendance sheet. They complain that her office is too far from the front lobby of the hospital, where they work, and they suggest that she leave the book with the coordinator of their unit, Mr. Abdul-Rahman, to shorten their trip. They won't sign in at eight but only whenever their daily tasks take them somewhere near her office. I rarely drop by her office at eight, for she herself is rarely there at that hour. On most days, her door is closed until late morning; she goes to meetings outside the hospital, her secretary says. On the days she comes in at eight, she asks her assistant to bring the book to her office, to catch latecomers and give them a scolding.

When she talks to us, her female employees—who behave in front of her but complain behind her back—Sarah hints that her position as the manager of Social Services was made possible through the relationship that her father, a rich businessman and shareholder of the hospital's royalties, has with the hospital administrator. In other words, her clout comes from "high above," not from her degree or managerial skills, which are not important at all. This link to higher authorities safeguards her job and preserves her authority; it is what matters to her. To protect her position of power, Sarah once commissioned a non-Saudi employee, a poverty-stricken widow, to report all she heard and saw in the department—a situation that got me in trouble one day when it got back to Sarah that Munira, a coworker, and I had jokingly referred to her as "Susu," mocking her coquettish style of speaking. We women also relish gossiping about Sarah's habit of inviting male employees to her office for a coffee for no obvious work-related reason, keeping her door closed throughout their visit.

Sarah seems to prefer younger men, for most of her visitors are under the age of thirty. None of us could find an explanation for their presence at work-related events other than their striking good looks. My friend Shaza bites her lower lip every time she spots one of them. "Where does she get them from, the clever woman?" she whispers to me.

I passed through the corridors leading to my office, which is away from the patients' wings and the familiar hospital smell. The food distributors carried breakfast meals wrapped in plastic, while the intercom called on employees to answer the phone. Before I reached my office, I met Faisal, a ten-year-old boy who is a permanent resident of the hospital, wheeling himself through the corridors. Faisal has a residency status because of his family connections; he is not sick, he is handicapped and in need of special care. His rich parents, who travel to Switzerland every summer, cannot see to his needs at home, even with the help of a private nurse or a servant. But they do have the influence to obtain a letter to ensure that he can stay for many years at the hospital.

Faisal was once a beautiful child, as his features indicate, but a medical error caused him to be mentally challenged and robbed him of his childhood.

"Good morning, Faisal."

He looked at me, trying hard to lift his neck, and smiled. I stroked his hair.

"Will you come with me? I have a biscuit for you in my bag."

Being shy, Faisal looked the other way. A nurse emerged out of the children's wing and called out to him. "There you are, Faisal! I was looking for you!" When she saw me, she said, "Good morning, Mrs. Hend."

"Good morning, Jane. How are you today?"

"Fine," she said, stroking Faisal's hair. The European Jane loves the boy more than his parents seem to. Taking the handles of his wheelchair, she said, "You need a haircut. Come on now, it's time for your breakfast."

I went to the office and found Shaza brushing her lashes with black mascara, giving her eyes a charming and mysterious look. Shaza is beautiful, with well-defined Bedouin features. Her black eyes gleam with eagerness and joy, and her small teeth crowd each other in untidy rows that lend her laughter a touch of youthful warmth and spontaneity. Meeting her, you might think that she is a butterfly in a field painted with stories of love and leisure. You might even wrongly judge her as spoiled and arrogant.

Everyone at the hospital associates me with my coffee thermos. I put it on my desk and remove the lid, filling the place with the heady smell of coffee. Anyone passing by comments on the scent, a thinly veiled request for a cup. I never deny anyone, although I am always ready to cut short any conversation that might lead to another cup by pretending that I have some work elsewhere, letting the guest know that coffee time is over.

I poured some coffee into the colorful porcelain cup I'd brought from home and filled another cup for Shaza, which I placed on her desk. Our holier-than-thou colleague Juhayr—we call her Hajja[25] Juhayr—came into the office.

"Oh, I have a beep," Shaza said, elegantly rising to her feet and looking at her pager. "It's from Wing Fifteen. See you later, Hannooda."[26]

"What about your coffee?"

"Hajja Juhayr can have it."

"May Allah, Almighty, grant us His forgiveness," Juhayr muttered.

"Would you like some coffee, Juhayr?"

"No, thanks."

"As for me, I need a lot of coffee to wake me up."

"You mean you woke up late?"

"Very."

"Then you didn't do the *fajr*[27] prayer!"

I looked at her, at her round, fairish face, her small, dainty features, and the severe look in her eyes. Her words, so humorless, made me think she was about to enter into a long religious lesson that would show her knowledge of the Qur'an and the hadith.[28]

"Yes, I did pray, but sleep is a sultan," I said.

I opened my book in such a way so as not to show its title, and turned my gaze away from her. But somehow she got a look at the title on the back cover.

"May Allah help us! What sort of books are these? Don't you fear for your faith reading these Western books?"

I told myself I shouldn't respond; she would find someone else to quarrel with.

One of our male colleagues dropped in. Sa'ad is a young man who shaves his beard and likes to talk to women whenever he is given the chance. He asked the Filipina secretary about the head of our division.

"Sarah left. Would you like to leave a message?"

---

25. The feminine form of Hajji (a pilgrim to Mecca). Juhayr is sarcastically called Hajja because of her religious dogmatism.

26. A pet name for "Hend," used endearingly.

27. Dawn prayer.

28. The hadith are the sayings of the Prophet Mohammed.

"No, it's not important."

He started to joke with her about the picture she had on her desk.

"Is this your younger sister?"

"No, this is me," she said, and asked him in turn, "What is 'water closet' in Arabic?"

"*Hammam*," he said. "You must be careful, however; there's '*hamam*,' which means 'pigeons,' and '*hammam*,' which means 'toilet.'"

"Oh God! How can I tell the difference?"

"The difference is—"

"*Masha Allah*,[29] Sa'ad! Are you going to give the lady lessons in Arabic right here? This isn't correct, brother! As if we didn't have enough trouble in this mixed environment. Be careful! Satan is there between the two of you."

I glanced at Sa'ad, who looked embarrassed as a result of Juhayr's sermon. But he said, "Good morning, Juhayr! You are here!"

To get over his embarrassment, he asked her about some administrative procedures in the department for one of his patients.

His question pleased Juhayr, who set out to talk with enthusiasm, forgetting all about the Arabic lesson. I tried to busy myself with my novel. Juhayr left when Sa'ad, who still didn't feel quite welcome, escaped, letting a peaceful silence settle over the office.

---

29. Here Juhayr is sarcastically glorifying Sa'ad's ability to teach Arabic.

Seven

Christ Recrucified is the novel I was reading. It seemed like a good novel, and hardly dangerous, until I heard the title uttered by someone else. My heart sank: Christ, crucifixion, and Kazantzakis are all unfamiliar words in this place, not to be pronounced. I put the book aside, annoyed with the man who had revealed my secret reading in such a loud and intrusive way.

He was in his thirties, tall and broad-shouldered, with a light-brown complexion. He wore a white jacket and a hospital ID, which marked him as an employee.

"Hello," he said.

I raised my head but didn't respond. He threw a glance at my book and smiled.

"A good novel?" he asked.

I put the book on the desk to hide the title and tried to think of something to say that wouldn't drag me into a conversation with him. He seemed to grow uneasy when he saw the closed expression on my face.

"Excuse me. Is Shaza here?" he said.

"No, she left. Would you like to leave a message?"

Without waiting for his response, I pushed the green hospital pad and a pencil toward him, leaving them on the edge of my desk.

"Good, thanks!"

"Not at all," I said, faintly smiling, before he left.

The man I had once loved was also tall, his broad chest brimming with love. This love, however, led to a fierce fight with my mother when she discovered the relationship one day—a fight I lost.

I met him through a friend called Mudhi; he was a friend of her boyfriend. At the time, I was young and naïve, and our relationship did not go beyond phoning at night and exchanging photographs. I would leave him my photos near our doorstep, and he would take them after midnight and leave me some of his own.

When I heard his car approaching, I would go to the outside door to leave the photos. Then we would spend long hours talking on the phone about them. Once, he wanted to hand me, in person, the pictures of his latest trip to London. I hesitated. I didn't want him to think that I was a foolish and easy girl. But that night my heart was starving to be with him. He came at one in the morning, when everyone was sleeping. My brother Ibrahim had gone away for an overnight camping trip in the desert. I asked my sister Mashael to be vigilant and give me a signal if she heard my mother's door open.

I put on a green dress with white flowers and applied kohl and lipstick. I waited behind the slightly open door, having turned the light off so that no one passing by would recognize him. He drove around the house a few times to make sure there was no one who could see us. When he saw the light flicker on and off (the signal we had agreed upon), he slowly drove to our door. I heard his car hissing quietly as it drew nearer, so I opened the door a little wider and waited there as I heard the car door being closed and glimpsed a white *thobe* approaching the door. My heart was racing, my mouth was dry, and my hands had started to shake. He came toward me with a brave smile. He seemed to be much more collected than I was.

This was the first time I had seen my love face to face. His eyes sparkled; his white teeth, too, seemed to show joy at our meeting. So did his white *thobe* and his voice as he warmly said, "Good evening, my love. At last!"

Everything about his presence blossomed with love. He looked alive and vibrant, as opposed to the stillness of his features in the photos, which I had hidden in a drawer in my room.

"Are you cheering for the Watani team?"[30] he said, pointing at my green dress.

---

30. Literally meaning "national team," al-Watani is one of the most important soccer teams in Saudi Arabia. The team wears green jerseys.

I smiled, feeling shy; my heart was beating so frantically I couldn't control my breathing. Every time I opened my mouth to say something, I thought I was going to faint. He gave me a small bag with two carnations sticking out of it and a small box containing a French perfume called Anais. My heart still quivers when I smell it.

The scent of carnations crept to my nose for the first time in my life. I had never seen real flowers. I knew them through school writing classes and also through Egyptian films and pictures of the weddings of my friends' sisters—in addition to the plastic flowers my mother placed in the corners of our house. Never before had a man presented a fragrant carnation to me as a token of his passion, which was as broad as his chest. I wiped my forehead; then I took my hand to my hair, now smoothing the front, now lifting some strands away from my eye. I brought my fingers to my cheek and smeared my blusher. In my nervousness, I couldn't look at his face or enjoy his gentle flirtations. I feared that my mother would discover us, my brother would unexpectedly return early, or my neighbor would suddenly appear—the one who had flirted with me to no avail. He would see the shiny car of my beloved, the only one around, and tell my brother about me out of jealousy. I wished my love would leave right away and let me go back to my room to swim safely in his love; loving him in private was much easier than loving him near our door. He wanted to stay longer, thinking that my shyness kept me from talking to him about our love, not knowing that I was almost choking with fear. He tried to come closer to me, bringing his face nearer to mine. Then he touched the beaded string hanging from my belt and started to fiddle with it.

"Would you please, that's enough! Go now," I said.

"Fine," he said, "but on one condition. I want a kiss before I go."

I almost laughed, out of sheer astonishment. "Really . . . you are very bold!"

"Yes, what did you think?" he said, pulling at the part of the belt hanging from my waist. "I'll have it means I'll have it."

I pulled his hand away from my belt with some violence, causing the belt to break in his hand.

"Oh, I'm sorry! I broke your belt," he said, apologizing, and he bent down to pick up the beads that had fallen on the floor.

"Don't worry about the beads! Go away!" I said, bending, too, to take them from his hand and send him away. At that moment he straightened, causing his head to crash into my lips. I was in pain, but it didn't matter. I just wanted him to leave.

"Oh, blood!" he said, looking at my lips.

I thought he was joking and raised my finger to my lip, which felt a little swollen.

"No, no! Wait," he said, grabbing my fingers.

He placed his palms on my ears and turned my head toward the light to see my lip, I thought, to examine the damage. Before I could look into his eyes to see his intent, his face had already shaded mine in a kiss.

Eight

〜

MY FATHER WAS A SOLDIER, simple and illiterate. He held the rank of first sergeant by the time he left the military. But he continued to be full of pride for his military past. He liked to talk about his work in an army battalion and participating in military drills. When my mother noticed the nostalgia in his eyes, she would bring up the story of his infatuation with a woman called Hend, a distant neighbor. She was the type who appeared in public wearing a veil—but just a flimsy layer of black silk to make her appear more beautiful than she was. Mother said he called me Hend because of his infatuation with her.

I heard the story a hundred times, and every time my father denied it. He said that he liked the name because it was not so common at the time. All the same he took pleasure in this rare display of jealousy on my mother's part, thinking that it was a sign of affection from this woman who never showed it.

"May Allah guide your thoughts, Heila! What is the use of this talk in front of the girls?"

Mother thinks tales of love are nothing but insolence and absurdity, unlike my father, the dreaming soldier, who doted on legends of love and spoke of them as splendid records of our history. He talked about chaste love in his village, which he didn't see as shameful, and went on to relate the story of Qays and Layla, heroes of the most notable love story in Arabic chronicles.

"Could it be possible that Layla al-'Amiriyya is one of my grandmothers?" I said to him.

"You may be one of her daughters, my dear!" he said, laughing.

My brother Ibrahim opened his book (*Minhaaj al-Sunna al-Nabawi-yya* by Ibn Taymiyya, about the Prophet's tradition) and put his face in it, shaking his head in objection to my father's tolerance toward the subject of amorous love. He grew so angry that he lifted his head to say, "I wouldn't be honored to be the grandson of Layla al-'Amiriyya! Poets are supported by deviants. You're all deviants."

"Who said you are the grandson of Layla al-'Amiriyya?" I replied. "You are the grandson of Musaylima al-Kadhab."[31]

Ibrahim leapt up and began pulling my hair.

"Help me, Father!" I screamed.

"It serves you right for your loose tongue," my mother said.

My father liked to lounge around in a lightweight green *izar*[32] with no undergarments during the summer. As he jumped to his feet, he stepped on the edge of the cloth and undid the knot that kept it in place. It had slipped almost to the ground when my sister 'Awatif began to laugh and our youngest brother, Saud, clapped his hands, thinking that we were playing. My father hung on to his wrap, trying to fix it, while Saud tugged at it to play the game one more time. Father kicked Saud away and yelled at Ibrahim, who was kicking my stomach.

"Leave her alone, animal!"

He came to us, freed my hair from Ibrahim's fist, and gave him a push that sent him crashing against the wall.

Ibrahim was outraged. "You have hit me for her sake!" he shouted at my father. "You have hit me, a man in the house!"

"If you were a real man, you wouldn't have laid your hands on a powerless woman. This is your sister. Instead of protecting her, you're beating her."

Ibrahim left the room, indignantly muttering to himself, "Just wait. I'll show you, and I'll show her!"

---

31. This is Musaylima the Liar, who claimed prophecy during the lifetime of the Prophet Mohammed and gained strength by allying himself with a number of Arab tribes. He was vanquished during the lifetime of Caliph Abu Bakr in a campaign that claimed the lives of many Muslims. To be identified with this apostate is not something that the very religious Ibrahim could tolerate.

32. A saronglike cloth worn by men, mostly at home, in the Arabian Peninsula and the Gulf region.

"Ibrahim is now a man, as tall as you are," my mother said, reprimanding my father. "How could you hit him on account of this hateful girl?"

My father looked in the direction of Ibrahim, who was taking his head cover from a rack in the corridor and throwing it on his shoulder.

"The idiot," Father said. "He does all this in my presence. What will he do when I am dead?"

People's lives began to change in the mid-seventies, when oil wealth began to light up the nights of Riyadh and polish the dingy city during the day. Glass buildings sparkled around us, and shiny asphalt overlaid the dusty roads. Money flowed in people's hands and dazzled their heads with dreams of wealth. My father was one of the adventurers. He opened a real estate office, following the example of those who knew that Riyadh was going through tremendous spikes in real estate values. During those years, he owned two big buildings in addition to a spacious villa for us to live in. He became a millionaire in ten years. We moved to the big two-level house, with a large garden, in the district of North 'Olaya, which would soon be a popular bedroom community. At the time it was new; there were hardly any houses. We had a servant and a driver.

My father's relatives mocked him for what they considered to be a thoughtless move. 'Olaya was practically a desert—far from the city limits—compared to our old neighborhood in the south, where houses stood close to each other, where most of our relatives lived, and where we knew all the residents. We knew no one among the very few people who lived in our new suburb.

Its inhabitants were eminent people who lived in new palaces. Some had been poor before the oil boom; many had owned no more than a small booth for money exchange during the Hajj season, which they survived on the rest of the year. These men became owners of distinguished banks and well-known companies in Riyadh, or they assumed important positions with one of the government organizations.

At that time our neighbors glittered with wealth and prestige, unlike our simple father, who came from the southern quarter and whose past carried nothing better than the rank of first sergeant. In ten years, however, 'Olaya grew into the center of Riyadh, a region teeming with people, and the south became a distant, hard-to-reach part of the city. We didn't see our relatives except on special occasions, such as weddings, which grew fewer over the years. Girls were no longer expected to marry at a very young age; therefore, a statement like "the girl wants to finish her studies" gradually became a popular excuse that embarrassed no one, told sometimes to undesirable suitors.

My father's gentle heart was fond of us girls, unlike my mother's, which went for boys. I could have discussed with him my desire to remain unmarried, had it not been for the event that metaphorically broke my back. It left me defenseless in the battle with my mother, who handed me to her nephew, Mansur. She knew he was her true successor, capable of absolute authority.

My parents' endless quarrels were our only outlet to freedom. When they argued, it was easy for me and my sisters, 'Awatif and Mashael, to get our father's consent to go to the souk. Our mother would refuse to join us because of the fight. Our joy was often short-lived; no sooner would we reach the car than she would follow behind, having already put on her abaya. She would sit in the back seat rather than next to our father on these occasions. At the end of our drive, she would whisper to one of us just as we were leaving the car, "Tell him to give me some money."

As soon as we did, he would say, raising his voice to make her hear him, "After all this bad behavior she wants money!"

Stepping on the gas pedal, he would leave us near the first part of the souk. We couldn't help laughing in secret at our mother, whose side we rarely took against our father.

She felt that he intended to provoke her by treating her this way, to humiliate and intimidate her so that she would succumb to his demands—especially his nightly demands, which continued to be made despite his age.

Sometimes she swallowed her pride and forced herself to satisfy them, knowing that she had to show him some leniency and cut down on her opposition if she wanted him to buy her a gold necklace or a new fridge. She didn't know how to flirt with him as other women did with their husbands; since their marriage, her body had turned into a stiff wooden pillar, and she wished she could beat him with it. He was the man who had robbed her of childhood innocence, of her village and her friends; she could not forgive him for what he did. How could she forget the first time he slept with her, when he had tied her hands and feet and preyed on her like the frightening, mythical afrits that haunted the well in her village? She had been rattled to the bone that night, and she decided to always hate and torture him no matter how long they lived together.

She had to give in to his demands every time she was invited to a wedding by her relatives. She felt the need for a new dress or a 24-carat gold necklace—not because she liked clothes or gold, but to avoid the back-biting of female relatives, who often scoffed in her presence at any woman who showed up with a wrist or a neck that didn't sport costly jewelry. They saw an unadorned woman as one whose husband didn't value her, one who lived like a servant, slaving away during the day and lying with him at night without getting so much as a gold necklace for her labors.

Heila was afraid that other women would know about her bitter and relentless feuds with Othman, and she did her best to show them that she was valuable to him. She didn't want to give them a chance to whisper about her behind her back or show her their false sympathy—the way they did at the start of a slandering session: "Poor woman, so unlucky!" Therefore, she adorned herself at every event with a big piece of 24-carat gold, which she changed at intervals—short or long, depending on the size of her quarrel with Othman. But she always paid him for it with a night in which she would turn her head to the wall despite her stomach, which roiled and heaved and choked her breath as soon as it sensed Othman's intentions. She forced herself to be patient till he was done; then she would vomit in the bathroom nearby. Othman would turn his head to the other side and ask for God's forgiveness and help, but the man inside him—his conscience—would mock him. "She doesn't love you, donkey!" Othman, however, resisted this voice, although he knew it was right; he didn't have the courage to deal with the problem. The man inside would repeat himself. "You are, indeed, the donkey your mother birthed." Then Othman would sleep, contented and relieved, as he did every night, no matter what happened.

Nine

WHO REVEALED OUR SECRET that day? Should I blame my unlucky stars or my mother's friend? She liked to snoop on teenage girls when they met in a private setting to share their little secrets: a handsome man who had walked close to one or a phone call made by another to a well-known society man—just to see whether he was, like other men, ready to flirt with girls and cheat on his women. All we wanted was the outcome of the call, which hardly ever changed. Then we would say in wise tones: "Men are all like that, traitors! They can't resist the voice of a female. They love to fool around." We also shared stories about all the young men who shadowed us when we walked home after school or in the malls. And there was the story of the young man who tossed a slip of paper with his number into the car of one of the girls. When the girl insulted him, he responded by telling her a funny joke.

These episodes were little more than teenage pranks, but some of the girls who came from strict families made them public out of envy. Occasionally, too, an older sister would spy on us and report us to our mothers.

My mother was in a bad mood that day (not that she wasn't always in a bad mood) after having a conversation with one of her friends—a pockmarked, cross-eyed woman who most likely related her daughter's report about me, revealing news my mother herself didn't know. "Pay more attention to your daughter Hend," she warned. "Allah knows what she might do!"

It disturbed my mother to know that despite her careful spying she had been missing things that she viewed as far more serious than her friend made them out to be in her story. She felt it as a mighty stab to her skills, craft, power, and control, and she was determined not to forgive herself for this slip. In her rage, she didn't listen to the rest of the stories woven about other girls in the circle. If she had, she would have realized that my story was a mere choral part in a long, absurd drama. She decided to leave the amusement park, our outing that day, earlier than planned, unable to wait till the evening. She set out to search for me, fumes of wrath dimming her vision.

On that day, Mudhi and I had arranged to meet her boyfriend and mine in the café next to the amusement park. The two were waiting for us when we went in. Mudhi and her boyfriend had a table to themselves in the family section, in which the tables are separated by wooden partitions, while my man and I had another. For the first time I allowed myself the pleasure of meeting his gaze, listening to him with my eyes, and studying his handsome face. Only shyness kept me from saying "I love you."

For the first time I was happy without being afraid. We talked for a while in murmurs. Then he told me, "You look like Salma Hayek; I've seen her in a video."

"And you look like Raghib 'Alama."

"Do you like Raghib 'Alama?" he asked me, laughing.

"I would die for him."

My heart gave a sudden leap when I looked at my watch. I stood up and called out to Mudhi from behind the partition: "Oh dear! It's seven o'clock, Mudhi!"

"Calm down, you crazy girl," she said, her sentence interrupted by a kiss. "It's still early."

"Not early at all. If you don't come with me, I'll leave alone."

I walked quickly. Hearing my shoes on the wooden floor of the café, Mudhi followed me. I realized that I hadn't said goodbye to my love, but time had run out so very quickly; I was afraid my mother would discover my absence. In my confusion I said to him, "Goodbye, Raghib."

Mudhi looked at him and laughed. "Is your name Raghib now?"

I heard them laughing, but my heart was pounding in fear.

My mother stood at the gate of the amusement park, puffing out her charred nerves like a train. When she saw me, she looked pleased. Her hunch had been right. It didn't hurt her that I had betrayed her trust; all she thought of was the tasty dinner in which the main course would be beating me. She wasted no time, taking hold of my hair and slapping my face. I screamed. A woman watching the scene screamed, too, and I heard someone say, "Poor girl! This is awful!"

My mother didn't say a word, grinding her teeth and hissing and groaning. I let out a louder scream, bringing more onlookers. By then I was quite embarrassed. I drowned my voice and, like my mother, ground my teeth and moaned quietly. Tears were running down my face. Mudhi had already slipped away.

"Damn you! May Allah end your life and relieve me of your presence," my mother said, pushing me into the women's sitting room on the first floor of our house. She locked the door after tearing my dress because it was sleeveless and throwing my silk shawl into the garbage. She kept me there and forbade my sisters to talk to me or even pass by the door. It was the summer holiday, or she would even have kept me home from school. The day was long and boring. I was locked up without a phone, a sister, or Mudhi. Recalling her, I started to laugh.

My younger sisters felt sorry for me. They passed bags of popcorn, Pepsi, and Kit Kats through the bars of the window. I asked them to bring me some magazines and a notebook and a pen.

I had enough time to revel in the scenes of my recent date. My mind escaped my present jail to dwell on the meeting, to feed upon it in the darkness of the day and enjoy the taste of the details I lived with him. I examined, with no fear or hurry, the face of the man, his words, his jokes, and his suggestive remarks. How did I remind him of Salma Hayek, a seductive actress who was known for her nude scenes? Did he mean just her face, or other features he might have mentioned if we had continued to talk? I buried my face in my hands, embarrassed about what he could have imagined or said. Closing my eyes, I dreamed about him, rewinding scenes whenever I felt bored. Sometimes I rose and walked around to act out the scenes that might have happened, adding details to the unfinished ones—like the last, farewell, scene.

"Well, I must leave," I say to him, getting up calmly and quietly and offering my hand.

"No, don't be silly, stay a little longer."

"Please forgive me, I can't; I'm in a hurry."

He keeps my hand inside his, and I feel its warmth and pressure. I pull my hand away, but he won't let go of my fingers. Perhaps the whole thing is natural to him.

"Come here, I'd like to tell you a secret," he suddenly says.

"What? Are you going to lie to me again?"

"No, I swear! I don't want anyone to hear it."

He puts his head under my black silk shawl, covering our faces. Then he kisses me.

Two days later an argument erupted between my parents, driving my father to say that Mother was full of distrust; she accused everyone in the family, even when they were innocent. He himself was not spared her suspicions. She had never been happy with anyone her whole life. Perhaps, he told her, her misgivings about me were wrong. Then he stomped off to open the door of the women's sitting room where I was imprisoned without looking into my eyes. My mother was silent. She was never afraid of my father except when he was angry, which was rare.

I wondered why my father had freed me. Did he doubt my mother's story? Or was he, rather, unwilling to believe it? Perhaps he felt sorry for my being subjected to her long, cruel punishment.

During the period I was locked in, I realized once again that writing was not only pleasurable but also easy. I felt at home in my cool, fortified cave; no one but me could find the entrance or discover its secrets.

Had it not been for Mudhi and my own weakness, this incident would never have happened. She planned it when we were adolescents, linked me to this man, and even fixed our final meeting.

Throughout the six months we knew each other, I had been alone with him only once, the night he gave me the carnations. Mudhi managed to meet her boyfriend several times in her own parents' house. She would take him to her room, where they spent the whole night together. Once, she told me at school that she had left her boyfriend sleeping in her room. He had fallen asleep after their passionate kisses and intimate touching, which didn't spoil her virginity; despite their wild desires, they were careful never to go too far. She knew that her family would not tolerate such behavior and would surely kill her for it. Besides, her future husband would divorce her and ruin her reputation. Her boyfriend was very much tempted to go all the way but he, too, feared her family. It had roots in a mighty Bedouin tribe that would not be satisfied with anything less than washing away the shame with his blood.

It was daylight before they awoke. Realizing it was too late for him to go, she locked him up in her room and came to school.

Mudhi was unusually bold; we, her friends, could never be like her. She had no trouble acting natural around her family while the man was lying in her bed, whereas I was easily exposed by my mother, who could tell whether I was speaking with a man or a woman on the phone just by looking into my eyes. I tried to fool her one time when she caught me talking to the man in our men's sitting room at the other end of the house. I hung up but continued to talk, trying to give the impression I was talking to a friend: "Yes, Mudhi, and what happened next?"

She snatched the receiver from my hand and put it to her ear. She heard the familiar dial tone and realized that no one was there. She threw the receiver at my face, but it fell on the floor. She fixed me with her eyes.

"That was Mudhi on the phone," I said. "She hung up because she was afraid of you."

My mother walked away, cursing all girls in this world and wishing them dead without any further delay.

Mudhi had nerves of steel; I did not. During the summer holiday, when her brothers stayed up until four in the morning, she was unable to see her boyfriend in the evening, so she asked him to come wearing an abaya and veil as women do; this way he could ring the bell and be admitted just like any female friend. He knocked on the door, having been dropped off there by his friend, the man I loved. Mudhi went to open the door and told her mother and brothers, who were having their tea in the living room, that she would be taking her friend up to her room on the second floor. He passed by them and mounted the stairs in his veil and long abaya, almost tripping over it. Happy that he was safe near the top, he quickened his pace and slipped on the edge of the last step. Mudhi's laughter rang through the upper hallway and echoed across the marble floor.

"What's the matter with you two?" her mother called from downstairs.

"Nothing, Mama," Mudhi said. "My friend tripped."

They went to her room and commenced their usual amorous dallying. He took off his *thobe* and hung it on her clothes rack. Then he lay on her bed and asked her to make some tea for him. She called the servant using the internal phone, but no one answered. In the end, she left her room and locked the door without taking the key. She went downstairs, taking light, happy steps to the kitchen. Everyone had left except for her mother, who was watching a TV show. While Mudhi was making the tea, her mother went up to her room. She was suspicious when she found it locked.

When Mudhi returned to her room, she found it unlocked. The man asked, "Was it you who opened the door a few minutes ago?"

Mudhi's heart fell to the marble floor and broke into pieces. She feared that it had been her mother, who hadn't been there watching TV when Mudhi carried the tea upstairs. But it could have been the servant who had opened the door.

The internal phone rang in her room. She picked it up, holding her breath, her mouth dry. Her mother's voice was weak and muffled but commanding: "Get him out of your room right now!"

Mudhi's mother lay in bed for several days, telling her sons that she was not well. Yet she refused to speak to Mudhi, who knew that her mother had been crushed. She cried at her feet while kissing them. "Mama . . . Please get up and leave your bed! Spit on my face, kill me, but say something to me."

Her mother didn't speak to her for a month. She was, in fact, unable to talk, being terrified of what could have happened to her fatherless daughter, whom she loved very much, if one of her sons had opened the door. He would have killed her and the man and gone to prison, perhaps to be executed. The thought of losing both her daughter and a son in a scandal terrified her. What if someone else harbored suspicions? She knew she would not be able to do anything about what had happened; she could not betray her daughter to her sons. But there was no way she could accept the event. She resorted to silence out of fear as well as anger.

Mudhi was fading away, crying at her mother's feet day after day. She wanted her to get out of bed and punish her, but her mother remained silent, unable to deal with her emotions.

"I wish my mother would do to me what your mother did to you, only to have her speak to me," she said.

Ten

SHAZA CAME BACK to the office and found the message left for her by the young man.

"Was he here?" she asked.

I looked at the green slip in her hand and realized that she meant the man who had written the note.

"Yes, and he left you this message."

"Oh, my dearest!" she said after reading the note. Then on the phone, she said, "Darling, how are you? You passed by the office and didn't find me! I had gone to do my rounds in the patients' wings. Are you still in the hospital? Good, you can come now. Hend has the best coffee—Arabs swear by it. Birds fall out of the sky when they smell it. I'm waiting for you!"

"Now I know what's behind all the makeup you put on this morning!" I said, looking at her. "Do you think I made coffee for your morning appointments, Miss Shaza?"

"Whether you like it or not!"

"How courteous of you!" I said, laughing.

I had barely finished my sentence when we heard a knock on the door and saw the young man who had asked for her an hour earlier. I was about to leave the office, to give them the chance to be alone, when Shaza said, giving me a push, "What do you mean? Why are you rushing off?"

"Never mind, Shaza; the coffee is there, the dates in the basket under the desk."

"Fine, pour some coffee for us, and I'll introduce you to Mr. Waleed."

"Hello, Waleed."

"Hello. You're the owner of the novel."

Oh, dear! I thought to myself. We're back to that subject again!

"Which novel?" Shaza asked.

"*Christ Recrucified,*" he said.

"Lower your voice!" I said, making them laugh.

"Why?" he said in a hushed voice.

"People here don't believe in the story of the crucifixion, and you have said it twice!"

"Your friend is witty, Shaza!"

"And well read, too," Shaza said. "She spends her day reading books. It's either *Christ Recrucified,* or *The Outsider,* or *Chronicle of a Death Foretold.*"

"Who do you like better, Colin Wilson or Kazantzakis?"

"Kazantzakis, just barely."

"He has a calm philosophy, while Wilson is occupied with the super-human. Both, however, are focused on God. Wilson likes to rise up to him, to talk to him while sitting by his side; Kazantzakis wants to dwell in God's forests to contemplate him."

"Ah! You've found someone who could discuss your books with you better than me," Shaza said.

When he left, she said, "What do you think?"

"A nice young man. Good luck."

"What do you mean 'good luck'? Waleed is my brother, silly, the son of my mother and father. He works at the hospital's engineering division in the building next door. He's here today because he has an appointment with the doctor."

Should I go after him to bring him back, to listen to him once again? Could I capture what he said a minute ago? Bring his words back to life, delve into their meaning and spirit, so full of awareness, like a clear, flowing river? Listen again to his voice, calm as the gait of someone strolling in a green forest?

My heart screamed so loud I could have heard the echo break on the rocks of the northern Tuwaiq[33] and rise up to the sky as it drew another breath. "Your brother?"

---

33. The arc-shaped Tuwaiq Mountains are a very important geographical aspect of the Najd region.

Juhayr came in, and the two of us fell silent. Shaza took a cigarette out of her bag.

"Sister, a greeting is a Muslim tradition," she said, blowing smoke into Juhayr's face.

Juhayr didn't respond but gave Shaza an angry look. She took something out of her drawer and left the room. I laughed but said, "Stop it, Shaza! Don't provoke her."

"Don't you worry about her," Shaza said. "She's already complained about my smoking to the manager. Now they are looking for a separate office for me. They promised to give me the small office in the area across from Wing Four, and when it's ready we will both move into it. You see, one man's meat is another man's poison. As for what Hajja Juhayr is doing now, it's all posturing and acting, nothing else. God knows what she's been doing. They say she loves a Muslim biologist from Pakistan who works in the lab, and she spends most of her time mooning around near his office. Haven't you heard the proverb 'Often, under the unseeing hide the cunning'?"

"That's not fair, Shaza! You meddle in other people's affairs the way housewives do."

"Okay, my dear! I'll leave you to your book and your boyfriend, Casanova."

"His name is Kazantzakis; Casanova is your boyfriend."

Eleven

‿〜

"MANSUR IS COMING by to take Mae on a trip to al-Zulfi, to see his mother," my mother said.

I went to my room to change my clothes and rest. I fell asleep to the sound of music coming from my tape player. It descended on my ribs like a gentle waterfall, washing my body and taking me to a long river, which stretched all the way up to white clouds. I passed through an old neighborhood I knew from childhood and saw the buildings of the old souk. I know the place very well, having been there many times with my mother when I was little. Mother always shopped there, coming out with several parcels for which she paid no more than half the price asked by the seller.

Once, she bought some skin creams, ribbons for our hair, henna for hers, a tea tray—she loved tea trays—and a length of fabric for my cousin Tarfa's wedding. She also bought three dresses, of the same fabric and design, for me and my two sisters, Mashael and ʿAwatif, which we happily wore to the wedding. Buying identical clothes for us managed to quench sibling rivalry, the cause of strife among us and headaches for my mother.

In my dream the walls of the souk as well as its shops had all crumbled. The people's homes also lay exposed to passersby. I walked in the area leading to the souk, for I wanted to buy an old tape of Mohammed Abdu called "Sari, Asawwitlak,"[34] just to experience the thrill this song used to send through my blood. A hidden alarm went off, portending danger. I ran toward a huge cellar that other women were running to. These women did not look like the women of Riyadh; they were dark skinned

---

34. Described as the "Artist of the Arabs," Mohammed Abdu (1949–) is a famous Saudi singer. "I am calling on you" is a translation of the title of his song mentioned here.

like the Africans who served in the city's wealthy homes, and they wore bright colors. I didn't feel I belonged with them; my skin and my clothes were both different. But we were all in one big prison. I realized that when I heard someone call to one of them to tell her that her detention was over.

All had served time there, but they knew they would be leaving. And they did leave, one after another, as they heard their names. I didn't hear mine. Looking at the list in his hand, the guard told me, "Your name is not here."

I have no hope of leaving this place, I thought to myself. *The African women have all left, and I am staying here. No one will know I exist in this place; no one will help get me out.* A tall young man came in then and told the guard, "Don't worry, let her leave; I'll be responsible."

The guard looked at me and said, "That's fine; just leave."

A hand reached out to hold mine. I sensed its warmth, as if water had been poured into my palm. I woke up to see my sister 'Awatif holding my hand.

"Allah protect you," she said. "Were you dreaming? I heard you mumbling."

"I think so," I said. "What time is it now?"

"It's seven."

"Why did you let me sleep so long?"

"You've hardly slept for thirty minutes!"

"Thirty minutes is a long time. You know, when I wake up in the dark, I feel depressed all night, just like being in prison."

The words reminded me of my dream and the black women.

"What an idea!" 'Awatif said, laughing. "Where do you think we are, sister?"

Then she said in a theatrical voice, mimicking the words of Yusuf Wahbi:[35] "We are all in a large jail . . ."

Mae came in to ask me, "Would you like to go with me and my father to al- Zulfi?"

"No, darling, you're going on your own and coming back in two days.

---

35. The Egyptian Yusuf Wahbi (1889–1982) was a prominent stage and film actor and director.

You will see your grandma and grandpa and ride a horse and see little lambs."

"Can I bring one of them here?"

'Awatif picked her up and gently nibbled on her tummy and arms. "Isn't this little lamb enough for us? Come, little lamb, I am going to gobble you up . . . Hum hum hum," she said as she and Mae left the room.

My mobile rang once and stopped. It was Shaza's home phone. I dialed the number and heard the cool voice saying "Hello." His voice and that of Mohammed Abdu converged into one song. I smelled something I knew well; it was the edges of my heart burning with passion. I asked if I could speak to Shaza, whose voice I heard singing a love song: "You don't respond to my letters; what will I do with the paper?"

"Could you come for a visit?" Shaza said.

"Sure, I'll bring my coffee and come to see you."

"Okay, the coffee on you and the chocolate on us."

"I hate chocolate."

"That's fine; we'll give you some dates, Najdi woman."

'Awatif asked me if I could take her, along with my mother, to Jarir Bookstore on my way out.

Twelve

❧

AT HER FAMILY'S HOUSE, Shaza took me to the outdoor guestroom, located in a distant corner of the garden, so that she could smoke freely, away from her father, who was in the living room listening to the news on al-Arabia.

Her father, she told me, was a well-educated man. Formerly a politician, he had become an important businessman. Shaza was reticent about a period in her life when her father lived away from his family. She usually said only that he had been absent; later, she admitted that he had been in detention.

I couldn't ask her why; I was afraid of offending her. But Waleed told me some of the reasons for this imprisonment. His father had been one of those who believed in the revolutionary and nationalist discourse that was sweeping the Arab world at the time. After a failed military coup, he was arrested and found guilty of collusion, the extent of which his own children still didn't really know.

He spent many years in prison, and he faced the death penalty until he received a royal pardon and was exiled to France. This was achieved through the efforts of an eminent tribe favored by the king that interceded on his behalf. He had to sign a pledge not to engage in any further political activities or publish anything about his former ones.

"My father," Waleed said, "is unwilling to talk about the roles he played despite his political awareness. Perhaps he fears that one of us would be drawn to his ideas—knowing how dearly one may pay for them, as he did. During his imprisonment, he suffered diseases he should never have had at his age. It must have been a bitter experience; it tires him to talk about it, especially to his children. We respect his wishes and do not refer to it, either directly or indirectly."

Shaza loves her father the way one loves an inspiring teacher, a compassionate caregiver, a provider of shelter, a protector. For his part, he treats his daughters as though they were delicate butterflies. He spoils them and respects their wishes, but he pushes them to be independent at any cost and supports their efforts to establish themselves. He responds to their demands and stands against those who upset them or would take away their rights. Shaza has self-confidence as well as an engaging presence, qualities that have drawn me to her from the day we met.

Shaza's father is not the kind of man common in Riyadh; I feel that he represents a rare species. I got to know him better on subsequent visits to Shaza's house, when I had the chance to say hello to him, as well as to her mother and brothers. They all received me as if I were another daughter. In Shaza's house, I have come to know a climate that is missing in my home. Clouds of affection float over everyone, including the parents, whose union stands in stark contrast with the tense and murky relationship my mother had with my father.

Shaza and I went into the tent, which was made of a thick red-striped wool that was supported by iron poles. It smelled strongly of lanolin on that day because of the light rain. The tent was bedecked with attractive Bedouin ornaments and decorative lights. A gilded dagger and an old hunting rifle lay inside an antique saddle hanging on the wall. In the corner where the hearth stood, rows of teapots and coffee urns were stacked on wooden shelves. A tanned goatskin hung next to the hearth, and the floor was furnished with seats and cushions covered with red-and-black striped fabric. Slender logs crackled in the hearth, their orange flames reflected by a nearby kettle of stainless steel.

Waleed was sitting facing the fire and talking on his phone. When he saw me, he got up to shake my hand.

"Hello, sorry I'm on the phone," he said, continuing with his call.

A large TV screen sat in the middle of the tent showing *Forrest Gump* with Tom Hanks, broadcast by MBC2.

Shaza lit a cigarette and sipped her coffee while I watched the movie.

Waleed came over to welcome me after he hung up.

"Do you know that your manager, Sarah, called me today?"

"Be careful!" Shaza said. "She devours good-looking young men, chewing on the meat and throwing away the bones."

"Why not? Bon appétit!" Waleed said, laughing.

"Good! Then ask her to take care of me, since you like the situation; I may even get a promotion."

I laughed. Looking at me, Waleed said, "And you, Hend? Want me to recommend you to Sarah for a promotion?"

"No, thanks!"

Just like the logs in the hearth, my heart crackled in flames, these kindled by jealousy. I wondered if Waleed was trying to make me feel jealous, so I took care not to respond to my heart, ignoring its questions. I took my gaze to the TV screen, intending to change the subject.

"I like Tom Hanks," I said. "Last night I watched *Terminal.*"

"This is *Forrest Gump*," he said. "I watched it at the movie theater when I was studying in Washington. Listen to how Forrest's mother defines stupidity." The subtitles showed "Stupid is as stupid does."

"I have watched this movie twice," said Shaza. "It seems to me that Forrest Gump succeeded because he was a man. A man is accepted in any society, even when he is challenged like Forrest. Isn't that true, Waleed?"

"It might not apply to this movie. The character lives in an American society, but his mother had to fight to prove that people with a handicap are not deficient; they're different only in terms of their abilities. So despite his handicap, Forrest succeeded because he was given a chance."

"What puzzles me," I said, "is that he's able to succeed despite his mental delay, while his childhood friend, the intelligent and sensitive Jenny, continued to blunder in her search for meaning in her life. She went to university, she traveled, and she joined a left-wing organization that fought for human rights. Then she started to take drugs and even tried to commit suicide. Are all intelligent people like that? Paying the price of being intelligent, while less intelligent people often succeed?"

"A person doesn't have to be intelligent to make it in this world," Waleed responded. "On the contrary, a brilliant and sensitive mind may well handicap its owner. When Forrest Gump was fighting in Vietnam, the leader of his battalion asked him why he was there. Forrest said, 'I am here to obey your orders.' The leader was astonished; he'd never heard such a beautiful statement. It seems as though life could be summed up as follows: your ability to obey the rules makes your life a great deal easier. Intelligent people may complicate their lives by looking for new and creative ways of living; they try to live by the rules they themselves make, those they see as better suited to their abilities. These rules may lead them to either failure or frustration and may delay their way to success. But this is a marked difference between them and average people.

"While Jenny was dying, she asked Gump a question that may explain her continuous searching."

"What's that?" asked Shaza.

"She asked him about fear, but he responded by going on about faith. Perhaps he wanted to tell her that faith helps to blot out the fear that lies within our souls, to pacify the existential questions that cause us anguish from childhood on and require a lifetime to resolve. Perhaps it's fear that destroyed Jenny. She tried to run away from it as she battled for human rights or disappeared in drugs. But she suffered alone, feeling lost and very lonely. Intelligent people can be cursed by the inability to adjust to others."

"Because they are better."

"No, because they are different."

"I think," Shaza said, "Grandma Munira had the most logical theory: 'You may run like a beast, but you won't get what is not destined for you.'"

"You can add to that," I said, "what Omar Ibn al-Khattaab[36] once remarked: 'Grant me, oh Allah, the faith of the elderly.' Unquestioning faith makes life more bearable. But if this faith were easy to get, it wouldn't be a quality limited to the elderly."

I could sense that Waleed had started to feel bored. "Would you like to go out for dinner?" he said.

"No, it's late for me. I must go home."

"Let's go eat and then take you back home," Shaza said. "Do you think we will receive a dinner invitation every day? Get up! Let's go."

---

36. The second of the four caliphs who ruled the Islamic nation after the death of the Prophet Mohammed.

Thirteen

I WOKE UP IN THE MORNING to the chirping of the birds congregated in the fig tree below my room. It was almost six a.m. The birds kept singing for half an hour, as though reciting a morning anthem to salute the universe. Soprano voices wove themselves into the song, rising distinctly above the rest. The birds sang nonstop, without a single moment of silence, none forgetting their role.

I woke up, light as a butterfly. I remembered the Chinese sage who once said: "I dreamed I was a butterfly; now I don't know whether I am a butterfly dreaming of being a man or a man dreaming of being a butterfly."

I felt like a child sliding on a cloud, falling inside its fluff, then flying to another cloud outside the orbit of this world. Cool air grazed my naked arms, where tender plumes had started to sprout for the very first time. I passed my hand over my arm and felt the growth of feathers on my skin: long, white, silky plumage that warmed me and promised me a favorable flight. I lingered in bed, holding fast to my new feather abaya. I didn't want to see it fall away; nor did I wish to swap it with the metal suit, the copper shield, and the sword of a warrior, just to battle on in a life I didn't choose.

Waleed's face was what I recalled when I first opened my eyes—the glances he had sent my way the night before at the restaurant. He would look at me, then give me a tender smile full of light and love for life.

Waleed's car stopped at the new al-Faisaliah Tower. The guard there opened the hood and looked inside it; then he asked Waleed to open the trunk. Recent attempts to blow up the houses and compounds of foreigners in Riyadh have sent the government scurrying to enforce extra measures of security, filling the city with police and checkpoints. Cement blocks guarded the entrances of all buildings likely to be targets of suicide bombings, such as the al-Mamlaka and al-Faisaliah skyscrapers. As we entered the elevator, Waleed stood close to me. I could almost feel the warmth of his body inside his white *thobe* and could almost hear his heart beating one inch away from my black abaya—a surreal image, in contrasting colors. We stood as if in a primitive scene, having arrived from a nebulous time and heading for an unknown one. Waleed pressed the button to the eleventh floor. A recorded female voice said in English: "Hello, you are going up to the eleventh floor."

As the door opened, we were received by a Lebanese waiter dressed in a black suit.

"Welcome, sheikh."[37]

I looked at the tables: a number of women sat together—some unveiled, some covering only the area below their eyes with black silk. The men sat on their own away from them. Rarely would a couple sit together. The groups were all men or all women. There were also no wooden partitions between the tables as in other restaurants.

"Deluxe seven-star restaurants do not have to follow the rules imposed on other restaurants in Riyadh," said Shaza. "There aren't any barriers or surprise visits by the commission[38] looking for unlawful meetings between lovers or intimate friends, or forbidding a woman from being alone, without a *mahram*,[39] at the restaurant."

"Does it mean one can relax here?" I said.

"Certainly," said Waleed. "We came here, Hend, so that you can be comfortable and have a good time."

His consideration touched my heart. For the first time someone cared about my comfort, brought me to it, and offered me the freedom of choice. Gratefully, I looked at him. He smiled.

"Where would you like to sit?" asked the waiter. "On the balcony or inside?"

---

37. The word "sheikh" is used here to denote respect and warm welcome.

38. Shaza is referring to the Commission for the Promotion of Virtue and Prevention of Vice, or what is sometimes known as the religious police in Saudi Arabia.

39. In Islam, a *mahram* is a woman's husband or a male relative whom she cannot marry at any time in her life, such as a father, a brother, or a son.

We chose to sit on the balcony. The bright lights on the railing high above the city of Riyadh showed the tops of buildings and stores, and the streets and cars below. The city glittered, constantly changing colors like a big electronic billboard. Moths flitted about the candles on the balcony. One came too close, erupting in smoke as it burned. Like the moth my heart was burning, having surrendered to the fire of love.

"Look! The moth is burning!" I cried, like a young girl taken by a spectacle she is seeing for the first time. I had heard about moths loving the light unto death and read about it in novels and naïve metaphorical writings that liken women who look for pleasure to these moths: lured to the light and burned by it.

"Stupid moth," Shaza said, trying to match the excitement I showed at the scene. "It watched its companions burn, and instead of fleeing came to have its own turn."

"The moth's attraction to the light is instinctive; I wouldn't blame it," Waleed said.

I asked him, "Do you like your work at the hospital?"

"Despite what people say about nuclear physics as a dry and heavy subject, I do find some pleasure in my work. But I'm not one of those who look for pleasure only in work . . . I like other things."

It was exciting to start a dialogue that would lead me to know him better. His openness was like a wide field bathing in the sun, green and happy and optimistic.

"Like what?" I asked.

"Like talking to a woman such as you: intelligent, educated, and beautiful."

"Hmm," Shaza said. "Am I to understand that I'm not welcome here?"

Fourteen

MY HUSBAND, MANSUR, is a cavern, having managed to escape the sun and remain in cold darkness. He has divided himself into many secret tunnels, none of which reveal the secrets of its neighbor. Each promises a chamber of wonders but leads to a separate dead end. Just when you think you've found the one true passage through the maze, a new tunnel will appear. Duplicity preserves Mansur's secrets, as if it were a part of his military training. I knew his love only in the cave's mouth, the chamber closest to the light. I thought it was a good hiding place, a safe station for two souls, a home for two individuals. I used my mind, following my mother's advice: "A sound mind is a gem, my daughter." The feathers of fantasy all fell off my soul, day after day, feather after feather, until I turned into a featherless bird.

I ceased to be the girl with boundless dreams when I became a wife starting a new life, listening to her mother's counsel. She said on my wedding night, "A wise woman would not have a different man every day. Your husband is your destiny, your good and evil, your happiness and sorrow. You settle for what Allah grants you. If He gives you a kind man, this is a blessing meriting gratitude; if He plagues you with a contrary man, this is an affliction requiring fortitude."

Mansur was delighted to have me. During the early days of marriage, I decided not to let him down, to rise above my distaste for dampness and dark, and to accept my position as the queen of his cave. But he pulled away from me after our first few months together, having exercised his marital rights and ensured my pregnancy. He slipped away. I never found him to be that way again.

His tenderness left, having fled to a secret relationship. I knocked on the chamber's door, but he wouldn't hear me or come out. I lost him in the maze. Sometimes I heard his voice, sometimes I saw his face; but I never managed to reach him or share his chamber.

When Mother had discovered my secret relationship with the man I loved, I was forced to yield to her pressure. "Don't even dream of being able to marry a man you've flirted with over the phone at night," she said to warn me.

She threatened that she would never let me leave our house except to go to university. It was important that I think of marrying her nephew, a man we knew, our kin, who was better than a man we didn't know.

"You'll be living in a jail from now on," she added. "No phone, no friends."

She also threatened to tell my father all the details about my love relationship.

"He won't marry you, you know that," she added. "His family and ours are not compatible. If you did, your uncles would spill your blood."

If my father had known, he would never have forgiven me for my unpardonable conduct with that man. My case would have been complicated by the issue of a mismatched marriage. I knew then that what remained for me at home was nothing but absolute defeat. It seemed that my feeble father had surrendered all his weapons to my mother, who became the real soldier in our house.

My marriage to Mansur was the only thing my father agreed upon with my mother in the history of their union. This meant that the windows of heaven were all closed in my face; nothing was left but to be buried inside a bottomless well. I realized that my mother had won this battle against me, that my war with her would never end, and that I had to search for a space a little freer, a little easier and more merciful, a little less loud or obstinate than my mother's fierce warring.

Mansur was a handsome young man, having recently graduated as a lieutenant from the military college. He could provide a fresh start. Even Mudhi—who had ceased to be a reckless teenager after her mother discovered her boyfriend and had started believing in early marriage— encouraged me to marry him.

"You're just saying you don't love him to guard against the evil eye. Who would ever say no to Omar Sharif?"

By saying that, she was also consoling me for losing the man I was in love with, whom we would not mention again, especially when we learned that Mansur was good at listening to my phone conversations. He would jot down some of the words I had spoken to my friends and leave the notes on the table. When I asked him what it meant, he would say, "It's nothing, a mere coincidence. The words came to my mind and I wrote them down."

Mansur had his own strategies, which were hard to detect. He did not directly attack his prey; he beat on her nerves till she caved in and admitted her guilt. He was skilled at circling around his prey, wearing her out till she banged her head against the wall and confessed everything. To be spared this torment, she would demand the severest punishment: "I am the one, I am the criminal, spare me all this, may God spare you! Punish me, execute me if you wish, but don't do this to me!"

He never treated me as a person with an identity and soul and rights like other human beings. He labeled me "You women," and when I got angry, he would say, "You women have tiny brains."

If I asked him questions about his private world, which sometimes made me curious, he would say, "These are issues that don't concern you women."

When I daydreamed of spending a holiday on a green island far away, he would say, "You women make frivolous demands."

I stopped seeing myself as a whole human being, just an atom in a dark cosmic orbit teeming with women who kept spinning till they rose up in smoke. I told him once, "Would you please talk to me as a woman, as the wife you have known, not as a world full of females?"

"Why? What makes you better than them?" He drew on his cigarette, a smirk of victory on his lips. He was happy to wear me down.

Because of him, what vexes me most in this world is being a woman. Because of him, I am sure that in our world men exist in a wide sphere where they can spread themselves and hide away from the cares of life and children. They have the streets on which to drive their cars, the cafés and beaches to amuse themselves, and private flats for illicit pleasure. On the other hand, women are enveloped by narrow traditions wherever they go. Mothers keep worrying about daughters not because they care for them but because they dread the shame of dishonor.

Shaza once said, "A man's life is a large seat made to fit his own measurements, while a woman has to choose one of two options: staying home or going shopping."

When I was young, I longed for school because it was my only source of entertainment. Men create homes for women to imprison them. With time women grow accustomed to the fenced-in space and start to like it, thinking that it is the safest place to be. The world beyond is full of beasts that would attack them if they went out, for men are ravenous wolves. In my country women grow old far too soon, ridden by depression and fear—of their own illness and death, of their children's illness, of the loss of a husband.

Growing old, for women, means being damaged and beyond sexual appeal. A woman's role is limited and her value shrinks over the years because she exists as a dependent entity all her life: on a father before marriage, on a husband after marriage, and on a son in old age. Thus it is easy for this male guardian to be her overlord.

Nothing can fill a woman's mind more than emptiness; therefore, it sags prematurely. The woman who thinks of using her mind in more varied ways ends up mad, spinning in a cage of emptiness.

The need to question has been with me since my childhood, and has often cast me on roads of doubt and bafflement, followed by anger at the sheer unfairness of this life. Men can sit at the head of life's dining table and eat a whole cake without a single prick of conscience, even though they are aware of the hungry women watching them eat. They argue that these are time-honored traditions, written down since the beginning of time. It is not men who came up with these suffocating traditions; men have merely guarded them and, over the years, have even enlisted women to the cause—women who have become even more vigilant than the men themselves. Mother is one of these faithful guards. When I asked her how I was any different from Fahad or Ibrahim, her answer was always the same: "They are men, you are a woman. Don't you understand?"

I didn't understand what "woman" meant.

"Does this mean that a woman is a creature without a soul?"

"That is the way it's always been; you'll have to accept it, as we have before you, whether you like it or not."

I found myself to be the more intelligent one in my relationship with Mansur, yet he was the one who owned everything. I had almost nothing; in fact, I seemed to be one of his possessions, a thing transferred to him when my father gave it up.

My questions overwhelmed me; I felt as though I were an odd mythical creature that didn't belong to this world, or a thorny plant sitting on the ground without any roots.

Not for one day did I belong to the world of *hareem*[40] where Mansur had positioned me. My desire to write became boundless, more pressing than ever before. When I wrote down my questions I managed to ease their pressure on my mind. Writing had a magical effect; it siphoned the muddle out of my head, leaving it quiet and free. Yet I never had the courage to shout in his face, "Yes, Mansur, I have something the women you know do not have: I have a spirit that rebels against your world of narrow and mundane desires, a spirit that won't desist despite the pain of having to crash, time after time, against the grate over your dried-up well!"

Every time I tried to get out, I found him sitting right on top, trying to trick me into believing that the sky was no bigger than the mouth of the well in which I lived. He refused to let me see what was beyond; in time, he thought, I would believe, like other women, that the sky was limited to the mouth of the well.

The worlds that have fed my mind, worlds of books and films and unfettered imagination, have taught me that there is always a wider sky— paralleled, no doubt, by a wider earth, filled with all kinds of humans with missions other than the jailing of free individuals. How I yearn to see this sky and to be in distant lands with all their fields, orchards, fruits, and human beings. I want to have a long and broad and free dialogue with people who communicate by using their minds and not just their wounded feelings, like the *hareem* in the kingdom of Mansur—women

---

40. The word *hareem* (singular *hurma*) has evolved to mean "women." Linguistically, however, it refers to the female as a sacred entity forbidden to outsiders, more object than human being. A man's *hareem* are the female relatives under his protection.

busy with having children, cooking large, elaborate meals, and looking for new designs of seductive nightwear to captivate their man and keep him in their bed. Terrified by his departure, they would try all kinds of remedies, old-fashioned and new, to keep their fear of being deserted at bay. They never succeed. Their life gradually turns into a nightmare, tortured forever by the horror of being abandoned, locked up inside their wardrobes and kitchen pots, where their souls twist and turn till they age in despair. Tears become their nightly routine, and no one cares.

I looked every day at the revolver hanging from Mansur's belt when he returned from work. My hellish desire to flee his well drove me to think of pulling the gun out of his belt and shooting him with it. But then I thought I didn't have the guts to see blood pouring out, not even my jailer's.

Fifteen

I RAN AWAY FROM HIS HOUSE four months after our marriage. I took my clothes, hoping that I would not have to come back. But the things I packed first were my notebooks, which I had filled daily with secret anguish.

After the marriage, my own secure, hidden cave—my writing—was discovered and its codes revealed. My guardian this time was not my barely literate mother but Mansur, who could read very well. He found it easy to break into my secret cave during my absence; I could see human footprints and other signs of forced entry. My cave was no longer safe. I must return to where I came from, for I had only continued to live because of the cave, which Mansur had violated.

In front of my family, Mansur put all the weight of our discord on one side of the scale, thus taking our conflict to a new battlefield. He traced the dissolution of our marital life to a single cause.

He told my brother Ibrahim, as well as my mother, that what I published now and then in the papers under my real name had made his friends joke about him in men's gatherings.

In the counseling session set up for us by my family, he told Ibrahim, "We live in a conservative society, especially us military men. The names of our comrades' wives and female relatives are unknown to us. I have colleagues who come from different backgrounds, some from desert areas, others from religious groups. These men consider the public knowledge of your wife's name a shameful thing and laugh about it among themselves just to demean you. Our military ranks put us into different classes. The man whose rank is below yours should never dare to put you down by laughing at you just because he knows your wife's or mother's name. Can you believe it, Ibrahim? Can you believe it, Aunt? Once, I heard a soldier below my rank tell other people just before I entered the room: 'Here comes Hend's husband!' And everyone laughed."

Ibrahim was overjoyed to see someone stronger roasting me, sinking a knife into my flesh, and peeling the skin off in front of him. I said, "Who told you, Mansur, you had to plead your case in order to have Ibrahim's support on the issue of my return to your prison? Don't worry. Your command is his pleasure."

I had barely finished my words when Ibrahim, ignoring my sarcasm, looked at Mansur while addressing me: "Hend, if your husband is not happy with your articles, you have no right, by law, to publish them."

The two were happy with this agreement. They talked about compensations, some of which were already in place. They said I was allowed to continue with my university studies, as though this right, which I had practiced before, was still subject to voting and discussion. But they wanted to remind me that nothing should be taken for granted; all depended on my compliance. Mansur promised to provide me with a private driver on one condition: during his absence, occasioned by his many trips, the driver's wife should also be in the car when I traveled to school and back. I shouldn't be all alone with the driver; it wasn't right to roam the streets with a stranger.

I went back to where I started, publishing under a borrowed name— there were no guarantees in this place, this island of sand. Every time I built a house, the wind would come and pull it down; every time I wrote something, the sand would bury it, wiping away all my tracks.

Then I stopped writing for a while in an effort to reorganize my prison and look around for a tenable corner where I could express myself. I found the computer. I bought a card that gave me access to the Internet, and I had an e-mail account where I locked up everything I wrote. No traces were left behind; all vanished whenever I logged out, just like the jinni in Aladdin's magic lamp, melting like smoke in the air. I was delighted! I had discovered a brand new code, impregnable; not even Mansur, superb reader that he was, could unveil the secret of this new talisman.

Once again my writing won, over my husband as it had over my

mother. I was stronger than both of them. I was the one who always tri-
umphed in the battle of my letters.

The new outlet within my grasp could not be touched by Mansur. No
one could ever take it away. Not even as they all united to boycott my
name, which I shared with them but was not to claim. It was a link in the
chain that tied me to them; I must not drag it through the dust. A long
chain of ancestors would point the finger at them, embarrass them, and
disturb their lives if others chanced on it. My name in the papers does
not refer to a writer with a long family line who has distinguished herself
by being creative; the name instead unveils the identity of a woman who
has left her sheltered boudoir and exposed herself to the outside world. A
woman belongs to the inviolable sanctuary of the family, which wouldn't
want to see its women advertise themselves; each name publicly exposed
drags with it the whole family, making it the butt of jokes by strangers
who would brazenly ask, "The woman who writes in the papers, is she
from your family?"

The man's mortification would make it impossible for him to tell
whether the question was intended to shame or praise.

My brother Ibrahim would say, "No, she is not a relative of mine; we
share nothing but the name with her family." He would blush and sweat
and come back home with an avid desire to spray me with liquid fire and
wipe me out of existence.

As for Mansur, he would say at the beginning of our marriage (before
he had encountered the mocking of his friends): "She is just a relative, a
distant relative."

He wanted first to gauge the reaction of the person who posed the
question. He found it mean and brazen, like a man who stared at your
wife, without any shame, in your presence. A man who reasoned that
because you let her unveil, he should have the right to size her up in front
of you.

That is exactly what had transpired early in our marriage when Mansur
did allow me to show my face in public, using only a black scarf to cover
my hair. But he soon noticed that men on the street or those who drove
next to our car would stare at me audaciously, their eyes assessing all our
movements. He began to be stricter, demanding that I cover my face

outside the house, especially after an argument he had with a young man who had stopped next to our car at a red light. The man had turned his whole body in our direction and fixed his eyes daringly on me. Mansur was angry. "You want to join us in here?" he snapped at the man.

"If you don't want us to look at your wife, cover her, brother," the man said with a sneer.

Sixteen

I WENT BACK TO MY WRITING, this time under the name of Hend Othman, adding my father's first name to mine, leaving out the family name. Once again Mansur began to look around, but he could find nothing—no hidden notebooks, no secret trails. He would switch on the computer after I had shut it down to inspect the files, but there was nothing to hint about my writings. *Where does this woman hide her things? I'm sure this "Hend Othman" is Hend herself. This is her name.*

He guessed that I had breached our agreement when he saw the name in the *Magazine*, a Saudi publication to which I used to send my articles by mail. Sometimes he openly laughed at my statements, implying that he knew my games, but he did not directly accuse me of going against his rules, and I wouldn't admit it either. So he kept playing the cat-and-mouse game with me, quietly and eagerly: preying on my nerves, watching me calm down, then ignoring me as if the issue didn't matter to him. I was almost driven to confess, but I chose to put a hold on my writing for a time, once again to organize myself and find a way to save my pen from the gallows of Mansur and Ibrahim and Heila. Assuming a name other than "Hend Othman" would help quiet his suspicions. And writing for a paper in the Emirates, which might not reach him, would be safer than writing for local publications that not only went to his office but attracted his full attention—especially the articles written by women.

My new name, Zarqa' al-Yemama,[41] received attention from literary

---

41. Al-Yemama is a legendary pre-Islamic figure well known for her keen eyesight, which was far beyond the capacity of the human eye. She was able to help her tribe detect approaching enemies. She married into a tribe that subsequently attacked her father's tribe and wreaked

clubs in the Gulf; it attracted comments from readers who praised my daring and fearless pen. I couldn't tell these commentators that I wasn't what they thought. Yes, I was certainly the woman in the papers, but I was neither daring nor fearless. I kept silent. After all, no one believed Zarqa' al-Yemama.

I often dream of running behind a car or a bus, or a vehicle like Mansur's, trying hard to catch up with it; sometimes it is a plane that is taking off just before I climb up to it. I manage to get in only to discover that I am in a different place with Mansur, accompanied by unknown women, some wearing the burka, some baring their heads. Once, a friend of mine, Hawazen, was with us. She and Mansur were intimately engaged in a conversation. Every time I interrupted, he ignored me and continued talking to her. I threw an empty honey jar at him before I woke up.

My life with Mansur was a honey jar that was soon emptied, full of nothing. With him I was a dwarf standing before an angry giant. I could only bite his feet, which blocked my way, controlled my movements, and determined the details of my life.

Mansur believes that a man should not be involved in a deep relationship with a woman. In his mind women are born for pleasure, not for love. It is also their nature to gossip; a free man should never trust a woman with his secrets since it is hard for her to resist the pleasure of revealing them to her friends. Besides, mixing with women on a daily basis can weaken a man and make him soft. Those men who are seen as failures are often taunted as being "brought up by women." Therefore, a man should minimize his contact with them. Their place is behind him. This is why their living rooms are always built at the back of the house, their doors always face the back fence, and their bedrooms are behind all other rooms.

When cities grew and men became wealthier, they also had more

---

havoc with its men and possessions. In revenge, her father decided to ally himself with another tribe and invade the enemy. He was warned about his daughter's far-reaching vision, so he camouflaged his troops behind tree branches, which each soldier carried in front of him as they advanced. Zarqa' al-Yemama was able to see the approaching "trees" and then the men behind them. Her people, however, did not believe her and thought she was being irrational. When the tribe was surprised and demolished on the following day, Zarqa' was blinded before being crucified.

engagements and less time to spend on taking women out for daily errands. They decided to place them in the back seat of the car, behind a driver, entirely hidden from everything.

All the veiling and isolation imposed on women by Mansur relates to one thing, which he himself has memorized: a woman is the snare of Satan, the source of temptation and witchcraft, which she uses to captivate men, turning those who yield to her into a joke among other men. Despite Mansur's seduction myth, I didn't tempt or bewitch him, nor did he succumb to my allure. But according to Lieutenant Mansur, a woman is bound to lose her charm and her power over the hunter once she becomes a legal wife. Seeing her face every morning is enough to render her a carcass, which provides no incentive for the chase.

Once, he came back from one of his outings—he called them "secret military missions"—and as I took his dirty clothes to the washer, I could smell his mysterious women. I realized that to be exciting to Mansur, women must not be readily accessible. Sexual desire was unknown to him in his wife's bedroom. Yet the more he set out on these "missions," the more suspicious and watchful of me he became. He would ask the maid about the duration of all my outings and the driver about the houses I had visited. Despite all these reports, and all the notes he left on my college stationery, his suspicions continued to blaze. One day he startled me by coming home, stealing in like a thief, as I stretched on the sofa talking to my sister 'Awatif. He put his gun to my head. "Who are you talking to?"

I dropped the receiver on the floor and ran crying to my room. I could hear 'Awatif screaming, "Hend, what's the matter?"

He picked up the receiver, listened to her voice, and hung up.

I went to my family's house while I was pregnant with Mae. Ammousha said to comfort my mother, "Leave her alone; these terrible pregnancy blues make a woman hate her husband."

My mother left me alone for a while, till the period of morning sickness was over. But I refused to go back to Mansur, and he refused to divorce me. "You will be suspended for the rest of your life; you will gain nothing by being stubborn. You will remain in my possession; your harness will be in my hand wherever I go. I will never divorce you."

Ammousha seemed to understand my anguish much more clearly

than my mother. She related several stories about women who left their homes because the husband was hard to live with. My mother responded to her by saying, "If every wife left for this reason, none would stay home."

My mother continued her attempts to curb me, but my spirit escaped her siege and rebelled against it whenever it could. When I started working at the hospital, I spent longer hours away from her. The salary I received helped reduce her dominance over me and made me less dependent on her. She and I agreed for a while on the time I should take to do my work or run my errands. Then we entered into a period of cold war.

At the time, my needs didn't extend beyond going to work, being in my bedroom, and doing my shopping, but whenever she could, she pushed Ibrahim to set his dogs on me. She hid behind him, feigning innocence and justifying his deeds as being the lawful rights a man should exercise over the women in his household, out of an instinctual drive to protect his honor. He wouldn't be a man if he didn't do that.

"Look here, Ammousha," I said to her, "*I* wrote these words in the paper; this is my name."

"Oh, Hend, the apple of my eye! Will you read your writings to me?" she said in a tender voice.

I read aloud. 'Awatif, who was listening too, clearly understood what I said; but Ammousha had a hard time making out the meaning of the words despite my efforts to explain each sentence. Yet she looked happy and proud of me. I saw a sparkle in her eye and couldn't tell if it was just a reflection or if she had recalled something that made her cry. When I finished my reading, she said, "Oh, Hend! You were born only yesterday! You have grown so much!"

"Wow, Hend!" 'Awatif said. "How is it you write so well? It's so beautiful!"

"That is not what Ibrahim thinks."

"Ignore him. Write under borrowed names, sometimes as Whisper from the Sea, sometimes as Clover of the Desert, sometimes whatever else."

"Is it my fate to always excel at the game of hide-and-seek? One mask at home, another at the hospital, and a third for social visits. I have to wear one even when I write. Writing, 'Awatif, goes against wearing masks; actually, it calls for getting rid of them. I'm afraid that having to wear so many masks will make me lose my real face."

"Then call Fahad in Canada. Tell him we need him to put Ibrahim back in his place and get him to stop meddling with our lives. He is our oldest brother."

I did not follow her advice.

Seventeen

$\mathcal{C}\!\mathcal{T}$

MY OLDEST BROTHER, Fahad, was our mother's favorite child. We nick-named him Yusuf out of jealousy because my mother doted on him.[42] Since it wasn't her nature to love, her feelings for him seemed too obvious. But her limited capacity for love made it hard for her to love anyone else. He was her firstborn and first joy, the ailing infant, the obedient child who would not disobey her, as we, her daughters, often did. Fahad was favored with things none of us received. Nevertheless, he grew up to be like my father: tender-hearted, peace-loving, and unwilling to engage in battles with others.

Mother thought that Fahad would be the man she would use to fight her wars and keep the household under control. She tried to set him against us and treated him like the man of the house. She wouldn't assign him trivial tasks, such as buying bread, which we girls were asked to do. She expected bigger things from him, like giving orders, cursing, and delivering beatings. But Fahad failed her on all these counts; he would not spread his wings like a hawk over her home and snap at the game birds. Instead, he flew away as soon as he felt the presence of his wings, to free himself of her suffocating love.

She wanted him to be someone he was not, someone who would distrust his sisters, rummage through their belongings, follow them on their way to school, shoo them away if he found them playing with boys, and pull their hair and make them cry on the way home. But he wouldn't.

He could not do what she wanted, as he was more like our father than

---

42. This is an allusion to the Qur'anic figure Yusuf (Josef), whose father loved him so dearly that his older brothers grew jealous and wanted to kill him.

like her own austere brothers, who had pulled her hair and put a stop to her reading, who continued to terrify her until she was a grown woman. Fahad was never alarmed to see his sisters playing on the street. One day he needed an extra player on his team, and he invited me to play. He wanted me to beat his friends at card games, and he cheered when I won, respecting my right to earn some money and keep it, too. When we grew up and I could no longer play outside, he bought me the books I wanted. Fahad was a tame bird, not a predator; he loved his freedom and wanted others to have it, too. After winning the morsel of love from my mother's mouth, he flew away.

Fahad wrote lyrical poems, just like his teenage friends. He liked reading detective stories and watched American films. For a long time, he played soccer and dreamed of becoming a famous player, but my mother hid his jerseys when she was angry with him. She told him that if he thought of taking up professional soccer, he would never see her again, that her heart would curse him until Judgment Day.

He had a notebook in which he kept a bedtime journal. It was my window to an existence I couldn't live. I would tiptoe into his room as he slept and read his notes. I loved him better than all my other siblings; his notebook allowed me to know and love his candid ideas and gentle emotions.

He left home when he finished high school, the first goal he had set for himself on the night he received his most humiliating punishment. He told me that his training with an American oil company would give him a place to live away from home. On that occasion he had come to have a smoke in my room. I saw the cigarette and asked him in jest, "Would you mind?"

I held it as though I was acting, but he let me put it to my lips, smiling at me in a puzzled way. I took a drag and then blew at the cigarette, scattering ashes. At that moment my mother came in. Fahad laughed; he wanted to tell her it was a joke, just a joke. But I was so scared I almost choked. Mother picked up one of his shoes, which he had left near the door, and threw it at me.

"What a waste! All my efforts to bring you up have come to nothing! I thought you were a man!" My mother felt completely let down; perhaps this was when she stopped counting on her sons.

Fahad hated violence, and hated it even more when he came home late one night to see my mother waiting for him. She smelled tobacco on his clothes and beat him for it. At that time smoking was unacceptable in young men.

He ran away in the morning and disappeared for three days. He came back only because his exams were about to begin, but he avoided home as much as possible. His excuses did not satisfy either my mother or my father, but they kept him away. When the exam period started, my parents went easy on him. To prove a point, he submitted the easiest exam paper, dictation, completely blank. He meant to show that he had failed not because he was brainless but because he did not want to pass. That was his way of punishing her for beating him that night.

He joined a Saudi-American oil company that prepared high school graduates for studying abroad after nine months of training. It was his chance to leave home. He had loved our mother so much that he didn't want to ruin all the memories of that love.

He spent his nights at the company apartment, avoiding home. Although we saw little of him during those days, we did not seem to miss him much. His presence was so gentle and unobtrusive you would not know he was there.

Fahad did not tell our mother about his plans to travel abroad, not wanting to go against her wishes in case she objected as she often did: "It's either me or soccer," or "It's either me or smoking." He was afraid she would say, "It's either me or going abroad"—despite the fact he usually followed his own mind, and she herself avoided reminding him of the choices he had made.

Six months after my father's death, he called her to say, "I have a grant to study in Canada."

I REACHED THE HOSPITAL at ten minutes to eight. A man in his sixties was waiting there, fretfully rubbing his hands together. He asked me as soon as I arrived, "Where's the manager?"

I looked at her office door, which was closed. "She hasn't come in yet. How can I help you?"

"I must speak to her; it's an urgent matter."

The Filipina secretary came in a few minutes later. I pointed her out as the manager's secretary and suggested that he leave his number with her; Sarah would call him when she came in.

"I'll wait," he said.

Shaza came to my office.

"Do you know that man?" she said.

"No!"

"He is Juhayr's father; he needs to speak to Sarah about something. It sounds pretty serious."

"Juhayr didn't come in today. Do you think something bad has happened to her?"

Shaza dialed Sarah's mobile number; there was no answer. I poured the man some of my coffee. "Is Juhayr all right?"

He had warmed up to me by the time he finished his coffee. Perhaps he thought that I would understand what he had to say, especially since I still had the burka on my face.

"Juhayr ran away."

"How?"

"Her crooked brothers helped her escape with a Pakistani doctor working here at the hospital. Her brother Duhaym came to see me last night and told me she'd gone to the States to marry this doctor. They all conspired against me. I was the last one to know about it. But I won't let it pass; I'll turn the whole world upside down over their heads! I'll take them to court! I'll get them punished."

"Calm down, calm down, Uncle. My friend Shaza will contact Sarah right now to bring her here."

The hospital phone rang, and Shaza answered. It was Sarah. Shaza said in a low voice, "Juhayr's father is waiting here; he needs you for something important. Juhayr has fled the country to marry Akbar, the Pakistani doctor. Her father is very angry."

Half an hour later, Sarah and Juhayr's father were talking in her office with the door closed.

News of Juhayr's elopement spread in the hospital like fire in dry straw. It filled the corridors with the smoke of gossip and slander, especially since Juhayr had worked until the evening of the day before.

All those who knew her were amazed. Her colleagues could not believe it at first, until Sarah herself told them about it after her meeting with Juhayr's father. Those who sympathized with Juhayr discussed the event with an unusual open-mindedness and tried to justify what she had done.

"Juhayr is a mature woman," one friend said. "She took care of her family, her mother and siblings, when her selfish father left them all alone and went to have a good time with a younger wife and new children. He didn't care about his first family or their expenses. It's Juhayr who brought up her younger brothers and helped each one of them until they were on their feet. They knew about her escape and helped her with it."

"What Juhayr did doesn't go against Islam," another friend added. "She was divorced and had the right to choose for herself the husband she wanted. Besides, Dr. Akbar is a Muslim man."

"This is not important," Sarah said. "What her father is looking for is the man who helped his daughter get on a plane without his own written permission. He thinks that one of her colleagues facilitated Juhayr's violation of the law. God help us! We don't want a scandal here! What would people say about my department? Women eloping with their lovers? This will disgrace our department! The good name of the unit means more to me than anything else. I'll go to see the hospital administrator! That's if Juhayr's father hasn't beat me to it."

"I swear to God, jealousy is eating her heart," Shaza whispered. "She would like to do the same herself."

I laughed, attracting a glance from a spying colleague.

"What did Shaza say?" she asked, winking at me.

"Shaza would love to be in Juhayr's place."

She laughed, thinking perhaps I was serious. One of our male colleagues said, "Isn't it possible that one of her brothers has given her the permission to leave?"

Sarah did not hear what he said; she had already left the main office and gone to her office, where she opened her handbag, took out her lipstick, and applied it. Then she pulled out her bottle of cologne and sprayed it over her clothes from top to bottom. When she left, the corridor filled with *Angel Innocent*, her favorite scent.

Waleed passed by our office. Shaza and I had gone silent, as if birds were perched on our heads.

"What happened?"

Shaza told the whole story. He received it calmly. "Honest to God, the man who facilitated Juhayr's exit will go to heaven."

"What?" Shaza said. "Personally, I don't put this undertaking past you! You are suicidal."

"I am suicidal only in love." Then he looked at me. "Let's talk seriously now. Unfortunately, I was not the one who helped her. But why are you two so distressed? And why are you angry, Shaza? The woman didn't do anything wrong. What she did was within her rights. It was circumstances that forced her to travel to exercise her rights in a Christian land. Don't you think this is strange?"

"I'm not against what she did, Waleed; I'm only against her acting and her posturing. In the name of Islam, Juhayr constantly played a role that infringed on the freedom of many others. In fact, had she been here now, and heard her story told about another woman, Juhayr would never have accepted it. She would've been the first to criticize and condemn her. Do you know that she had a daily routine that she religiously adhered to and thought she would be rewarded for in paradise? She read the papers every day and marked the articles written by those she would call "secularists." She raised complaints about them to the Council of Senior Scholars and asked them to interfere in order to rescue the minds of the youth from ruin. She was helped by a doctor with a long beard, who sometimes came to see her in this office. I've heard them talk about the responses of some of these sheikhs."[43]

"How can you be sure that she actually acted on these evil plans?"

"One day she talked about an article by a writer named Abdullah bin Bkheit. I told her I had never read it and would like to see it if possible. She brought it to me with a number of others by the same author. Apparently

---

43. Members of the Council of Senior Scholars.

she was making a separate file for this man. The first article had this comment attached to it: 'A clear call to liberate women. Muslim brother, do
step in to renounce this thinking. Contact the newspaper's office and
the Council of Senior Scholars. May Allah reward you!' Another article
had these comments: 'To His Eminence, our Sheikh, God preserve him.
Peace be upon you. This is for your kind attention. I would like to let your
Eminence know that we have already spoken to them. Yours faithfully,'
with her name signed below. On a third piece she had written, 'Brother
Omar, please read this article and let us work together to stop this writer
from going too far.'"

Juhayr, it seems, forgot sometimes about her notes condemning writers who push for legitimate rights, such as empowering women in our
society or improving education. Sometimes she used the hospital's fax
machine to send her messages and the copier to Xerox the articles and
her own reports on them. But she used her mobile to send her snitch-
ing to a list of names she had saved there. I once received one of these
messages. It was about a writer who suggested using the science obser-
vatory, instead of the naked eye, to see the Ramadan or Hajj crescents.
In her opinion, the article had trespassed on the authority of the Council
of Senior Scholars; it was not right for an unqualified person to discuss
this kind of topic publicly—the writer was a university professor. This
message perhaps reached me by mistake, or maybe she thought I would
suddenly rise up to defend Islam. Why did she think she was entitled to
exercise her rights while she damned all those who thought of getting a
quarter of what she seized: escaping the country, traveling abroad without a guardian's permission, and getting married to a Pakistani—even if
he was a Muslim?

Eighteen

THE SUN HAD SET by the time I left the hospital at six that winter evening. A draft of cold air chilled my face in the silence around me. The lights in the white-painted foyer depressed me for no obvious reason. My mobile phone rang a few times, but when I answered, no one responded. At home, my mother was praying on her mat. Soon she concluded her prayer, turning her head to the right and left. "Peace be upon you and the mercy of Allah. Peace be upon you and the mercy of Allah."[44]

"And unto you also peace and the mercy of Allah," I responded. "Is Mae sleeping? I don't see her here."

Mother had a gloating look in her eyes. I knew this look, which she flashed whenever she thought she had caught us in the act: a strange glance, a mixture of sadness and joy, pleasure and pain, triumph and defeat. It was so complex as to be hard to comprehend, even by its possessor, as if a man were enjoying a dagger being thrust into his heart only because he could meet his killer's eyes and say to him, "I have caught you in the act of murdering me."

"May Allah wipe out all the girls in this world!" she said, and started another prayer.

I felt distressed. I wasn't troubled by the evil wish she threw at me but by what was hiding behind it. She wouldn't dare curse me again unless there was a disastrous event on the horizon. My cheeks burned, as though they had just been slapped; my body felt the fever it had under her beatings. Since my marriage, she had stopped addressing me in this

---

44. In Islam, this is called *tasleem* or salutations, and it is performed at the end of each prayer.

blatantly violent language. The ground had been cleaved between us so deeply that I no longer heard her wounding words. She was especially careful with the way she talked to me after I started working at the hospital and no longer needed her money. What could make her speak to me in this way?

I went to my room but Mae was not there. Nor was she in 'Awatif's room.

I sat in the living room waiting and thinking. My mother left me prey to anxiety, as if she wanted to add to my misery. She was facing the Qibla,[45] praying, while I sat looking at the silent TV[46] without seeing the pictures.

A loud, fragmented scream rang in the front yard. Mae came in, and as soon as she saw me, she ran toward me and buried her head in my lap, crying and shaking. Ibrahim followed, pulling 'Awatif by the hair.

"Leave me alone!" she cried. "Leave me alone, I said. You believe them, but you don't want to believe me."

"Why should I believe you, bitch? Everything is clear now!"

He pushed her to the floor, but she didn't completely fall. She landed on her palms to protect her knees from hitting the ground and sprang to her feet. He was about to kick her when she ran to her room. At that point, my mother finished her prayer and followed Ibrahim, who was dashing for 'Awatif's room. I held Mae and ran with her, while Ibrahim continued to scream, breaking the silence of the night. "Open the door, animal, or I'll break it!"

I switched on the air conditioner and turned the TV to one of Mae's cartoon shows while I changed her clothes.

"What happened?" I asked her.

"I saw Uncle Majid talking to Aunt 'Awatif."

I realized that Majid was the young man 'Awatif had met through the Internet chat room, the one she had started to talk to on the phone.

"Then what happened?"

"A man came. He had a long beard. He put his hand on Majid's hand

---

45. The Qibla is the center of the Holy Mosque in Mecca and the direction that Muslims face when they pray.
46. The TV is muted out of respect for the prayers that Hend's mother is performing.

and pulled him away, and spoke to 'Awatif in a loud voice; then he took us all in a big car."

In the morning, 'Awatif told me about the stormy evening she and Majid had spent at the central office of the Commission for the Promotion of Virtue. "I hadn't been in the bookstore for two minutes—I went to get a CD from Majid, songs he had compiled for me from the Internet. I stood next to the children's books; Mae was looking at the bright covers, picking one story then putting it down to pick another. Majid arrived, but he didn't shake my hand; we were afraid. So he stood next to me, and the two of us talked quietly. It hadn't been two minutes when one of the commission's men came toward us like a hawk—the wings of his black cloak flying about him, he was moving so fast. I stiffened with fear when he stared into my eyes. My legs froze; I didn't do or say anything, I just felt the darkness of his cloak falling upon me. Majid was very confused; the man had shot him the same dark, cryptic, and poisonous look, freezing his prey and making it yield to all his demands. The man said, 'Come with me.' We walked with him, while a soldier, silent like him, walked behind us. Mae asked me as she followed us, 'Why do we have to go, Aunt 'Awatif? I haven't finished yet!' As we went down the escalator, the commission's man looked over to the Islamic book section at the Egyptian employee, who looked back at him as if to say everything had gone well."

The following day Majid would tell 'Awatif that the Egyptian man was a spy who contacted the commission to report what he suspected was a date. Unfortunately, one of their cars had been patrolling a nearby street, so they came right away.

'Awatif was told a lot of lies at the commission's headquarters. One man said, "Confess! Your boyfriend admitted everything, and we have let him go. He said that he had met you several times in a private apartment."

"They asked me to confess! What would I confess when nothing had happened? But they said, if I signed the confession and penitence form, they would let me go home and keep the whole thing confidential; they wouldn't let my family know about the incident. All this was happening while Mae was looking at me and crying. I signed the form. I wanted to go home. I didn't want any problems. I declared that I'd never plan to meet Majid again. But as soon as they pulled the paper from under my hand, one of them signaled to the other: 'Get in touch with her brother, and tell him the details. He must see her admission of guilt.' When Ibrahim came, they took him to the manager's room and told him the same made-up story. He believed their lies and asked me to admit that what he'd heard was true."

Majid was young, but he refused to accept the humiliation that the Egyptian employee had brought down on him and 'Awatif. On the following day, he decided to avenge himself. He and some friends followed the man when he left the bookstore at ten until he drove into an empty street. They pulled him out of his car and beat him up.

"Stop getting people in trouble by spying for the commission!" Majid told him, as he delivered an angry blow.

"I was forced to do it, sir; I didn't choose this kind of work. I was told if I didn't comply I'd be deported! They would somehow set me up and send me away. I have kids to support. I'm here to find my bread—many mouths to feed, sir."

"Look for something else to do, more honest than spying on people," Majid said.

They left him crying, complaining to God about all Saudis, their filthy land, and the miserable day that brought him here.

Nineteen

ﻙﻥ

IBRAHIM WAS NOT YET EIGHTEEN. He was the middle child of six and not my mother's favorite as Fahad was. She didn't get excited to see him subdue her daughters with his stick or undertake his father's role as a watchman for her household. Perhaps she feared that the outcome would be the same as with Fahad, whom she had spoiled and fed with a love she wouldn't offer anyone else, only to see him let her down despite her efforts. She was sure her husband had not been strong enough to father real men; all he could beget were men who bore a resemblance to him: weak, puny, and soft with women—the way he handled his own daughters, listening to them, loving them, defending them, and fulfilling their demands.

Ibrahim encountered more neglect and bad luck than anyone else in the family. His being male did not secure him my mother's love; and since he was not female, he did not win my father's kindness. Nor did we, the three willful daughters, who grew up on fighting, give him the chance to dominate us—Mother was more than enough. Therefore, it was hard for Ibrahim to exert his manhood, even over his female siblings. He lived completely marginalized at home. My father tried to take advantage of Ibrahim's weakness and middling status to make him do chores related to his own work. Mother wouldn't let her husband make Fahad run his errands, for the boy had to pay due attention to his schoolwork. Yet for some reason, she didn't extend this protection to Ibrahim. At a young age, he was commissioned to help our father with his business, either delivering contracts to clients or working in the office after school, even during exam days.

He often cried to see himself saddled with duties while Fahad had the freedom to play soccer and stay out in the evening. Mother didn't seem to care about him, as she did about Fahad; she was also busy with Muhsin, her infant son. She, uncharacteristically, left Ibrahim to my father's control, and he took advantage of the boy's bad luck and powerlessness. He dragged him along wherever he went, even to the dawn prayer at the mosque. He would pull him out of bed to make him pray.

Ibrahim prayed out of coercion, not piety, but he won the attention of the mosque's imam, who liked the boy's righteous behavior. He watched him closely and gave him the attention no one else had. One day he shook hands with Ibrahim, as he would with an older man, after the 'asr prayer, praising his rigor and devotion to prayers.

"Which year are you, Ibrahim?" he asked him.

"Intermediate school."

"Take this book, read the passages I have underlined in pencil, roughly a page and a half, and practice saying them. I want you to read it well during the lesson that goes with the 'asr prayer tomorrow."

Ibrahim came home holding the book. He was filled with a pride he had never experienced before. For the first time, someone had made him feel important and addressed him as a man. That night he stayed up late as he read, memorized, and enunciated his speech until he was able to mimic the imam's performance: emitting the sounds through his nose, rather than his throat. He felt happy with himself. And when he recited the assigned speech, the whole neighborhood heard his voice through the mosque's loudspeakers. My mother and father smiled as they heard his voice, without being able to make out all his words, which didn't come out very clear. The neighbors, too, heard his voice, along with his friends in our area. That day he was as proud as a peacock as he walked in our neighborhood, where everyone showered him with praise: "Excellent, Ibrahim! Allah bless you!"

"*Masha Allah!* You are such a wonderful boy!"

"Allah guide all your steps!"

"Your parents must be glad to have you!"

Ibrahim tasted the pride that comes from being noticed after being marginalized, and he relished it. He loved this lesson, which made him the center of attention, and he decided to guard this position with his life even if death were to fight him for it. He was grateful to the imam, who began to depend on him for delivering not just the lessons but also the call to prayer; Ibrahim became attached to him and hastened to fulfill all his requests. At home we began to hear his voice every afternoon, coming from the mosque's speakers, which transmitted the first and second calls to prayer, as well as the religious speeches.

The person most interested in seeing Ibrahim was Jawza', the eldest daughter of our Bedouin neighbor. She had the habit of standing near her door, which she left slightly open to keep an eye on passersby. She talked to the younger girls playing in the street and sent them to buy her sweets, sandwiches, or juices. One day she saw Ibrahim standing near our door. With a signal from her hand she brought him closer and opened the door a little wider. He saw Jawza', who was five years older than him: he saw her short and plumpish figure, her rosy cheeks and kohl-lined eyes. Her smile captivated his heart. He wasn't sure what to make of the invisible tremors in his body and was about to run away when she stretched her hand to him with a riyal and asked him to buy her a chilled can of Pepsi.

"Buy yourself one, too," she said.

"No, thank you, I don't want any."

Ibrahim flew to the store, his heart trilling, his wings keeping him off the ground. The more he felt this feeling in his heart, the farther it traveled through the rest of his body.

When he gave her the Pepsi can, he felt the warmth of her hand, which deliberately touched his with groomed, red-varnished, shining fingernails. She pulled him to her, pinched his cheek, and gave him a kiss, all in a second that passed like lightning, but that electrified Ibrahim, paralyzed him, and set a fire inside his body. The smoke that rose to his head left behind a burning heart.

Jawza' wouldn't let go of him. Whenever his slight figure appeared, Jawza' was there waiting for him near her door. He himself frequently went out on purpose to see her standing there.

He was walking home on a nice autumn evening, which calmed people's hearts and houses alike. Just before he reached our house, he glanced aside, as was his custom, to see if Jawza' was standing near her door. She did not disappoint him. He found her in the same place; she had turned the light off so that no one would see her there. This time, however, she had planned for more than just a glance. As soon as she spotted him, she stuck her hand and half of her head out of the door and whispered, "Come."

She ran ahead of him to the stairs leading to the rooftop terrace, but he continued to stand near the door, frozen with fear. She came down and pulled him inside. Finding himself in the house, he went with her, abandoning himself to the thrill of the moment. The adrenaline pumping through his blood made everything look very different. Jawza' took him to the terrace, where the darkness swaddled his heart, which throbbed and leapt with sheer excitement at the pleasure to be tasted for the first time. The two went to a room in the corner of the terrace, which looked like a storage space for odds and ends. She placed her hands against his cheeks, frozen with fear, and lodged in his lips a few hot coals that kindled a fire in his face, turning his ice into moisture in her hands. On that night, Ibrahim discovered that love didn't come from the heart, as they say. The heart was simply an electric generator that pumped the first drops of love into the blood. They ended up in another place, gushing as a hidden thrill that penetrated his bones, quivered in his vitals, and then went down to his limbs before it bled into his underwear.

When Ibrahim came home that evening, he went to the bathroom and took his time washing himself. He spent much of that night locked up there with the water running. My mother banged on the door and shouted at him. "Are you blind! A river would run dry with all this washing!"

Mother said she saw him leave the bathroom just before the dawn prayer; she thought he must have slept there. But long baths and roaring water became his companions whenever he went to wash himself.

He was often absent from home, engaging himself in extracurricular activities in the evening and participating in youth camps, where he also spent the night during weekends. My mother was not comfortable with all these activities and trips, which kept her son away from home for long periods of time; my father was annoyed because he couldn't use the boy for his work purposes. But they had no power to ban his outings.

Ibrahim cried and complained to his teachers, who kept visiting my parents after every 'asr prayer to convince them that it was wrong on their part to prevent their son from participating in activities that aimed to propagate deeds of goodness, righteousness, and piety; nor was it right to keep him away from group discussions of dhikr[47] and hadith, for which God rewards the participant. Instead, they should encourage his endeavors. One teacher told my mother that such classes involved reciting the Qur'an, studying religion, and practicing judo. In the summer, Ibrahim went on trips that often stretched to ten days, during which his group went to Mecca to do 'Umrah or Hajj[48] before they headed for the Prophet's mosque. With the little money Mother had reluctantly given him, he would buy prayer beads for my father and a prayer mat or a can of Zamzam water[49] for my mother.

Ibrahim also bought religious tapes that dwelt on death; the torture of hell; the problems afflicting people living in our strange times, which would soon come to an end; and the fast-approaching Day of Judgment, the signs of which were already clear. Most of the tapes dealt with women: their temptation of men and evidence of their corrupt natures. Jahannam[50] is fed mostly with women, the tapes warned, due to their loose tongues and efforts to lead their male companions astray. These cassettes added to my mother's depression, increasing her silence and making her less inclined to visit the neighbors. She didn't want to come back with a load of sins on her shoulders.

She undertook a new mission: preparing her household to walk on the Straight Path to save them from the impending hellfire. She threatened us, for every small lapse, with the fire fueled by people and stones. Even the youngest of us began to worry about this hell; we lived in fear of Allah's wrath.

---

47. Dhikr means "the remembrance of God," and is the act of reflecting on God's attributes.
48. Both 'Umrah and Hajj refer to forms of pilgrimage to Mecca. The first, also called the "lesser Hajj," can be done any time of the year and entails fewer rituals than the second.
49. Water from a well called Zamzam located in Mecca, right inside the Holy Mosque. In Islam, the well is considered holy for its connection to the arrival in the city of Hajer (Hagar) and her infant son, Ismail (Ishmael).
50. Hell.

The word "mercy" dropped from my mother's vocabulary; it was as though her current mission served as a convenient vent for the perpetual fumes of her anger, which hardly differed from the inferno she predicted for all of us. She followed everyone around with orders to pray, shaking the house with her screaming and frightful pounding on our doors: "Wake up! You will be *jahannam*'s fuel!"

She also broke music tapes wherever she found them: around the house, in our rooms, or inside the tape player, which she used to listen to her religious tapes. 'Awatif would hide hers in her dresser drawers, which she locked. Mother also took to fasting every Monday and every Thursday. To her chagrin, this required my father's permission, since a woman's husband must allow this Sunna.[51] He felt that her religious bent had started to soften her to him. He took advantage of this weakness to press for her submission to his nightly desires, for the woman who declines her husband's calls will be cursed by the angels.

Ibrahim gained more confidence, but he grew morose as he copied his camp teachers in their speech as well as their sobriety and poise, making himself appear much older than his years. He hated the arts—including poetry, fiction, plays, movies, and songs—and he objected to celebrations and lavish spending, turning his soul into a ghost town. He pushed to change his own life and those of others into one eternal fast. Unable to fully experience his adolescence, he developed a fear of women. He trembled and scurried away when the maid happened to walk in front of him; he even shivered when a sister sat next to him. Satan, he felt, would be quick to infiltrate his mind if he were to let down his guard even for a moment. In the end he stopped mixing with all women, including his sisters and his aunts. He feared his body. Once, he told my sister 'Awatif that his teacher had warned the class not to take off their undergarments while showering; the angels, he said, would laugh at them. 'Awatif agreed with him; she had heard the same remarks from her own teacher.

Returning from ten days at a youth camp over spring break, Ibrahim parked at our door and noticed strings of bright lights festooning the front yard of Jawza's house. The empty lot across the street was covered

---

51. Optional fasting.

with red carpeting, and in a nearby dusty space, a man tended a blazing fire next to a row of coffee urns and tea carafes. A crowd of men, including Jawza's father and younger brother, stood near the door talking to each other. It tugged at his heart to see a wedding at Jawza's house; he knew that she was the eldest.

When he came in that day, his clothes reeked of wood smoke, and his face was deeply browned by the desert sun. He tossed down his bedroll, tied up with woolen ropes, and went to kiss Mother's head.

"You smell like a goat pen," she said, pushing him away.

Mother rarely dresses up, but when she does, she turns into a different woman: beautiful and mild. Her smiles could make us forget that she was the same woman who yelled all the time. Ibrahim noticed her jewelry and her dress, brocaded with golden threads; he watched her put the incense burner under her clothes to perfume herself.

"Where are you going, *insha Allah*?" he asked.

"To our neighbors'. Their daughter Jawza' is getting married to her cousin Dhaydan."

He coughed as he heard her last sentence. She moved the incense burner away from him. "Move away. You may be allergic to it."

He stayed, making himself cough more. His coughs were like indistinct sobs; they muffled the sound of weeping in his heart. Tears streamed from his eyes, causing my mother to laugh at him. "I told you to go away!" she said. "You will suffocate."

Mother had no idea the kind of tears his eyes were shedding; nor, perhaps, did Ibrahim himself. But he felt a little better with each cough and tear. His face and his red, teary eyes, choked with incense smoke, were yet another aspect of himself he wanted no one to see, not even himself, especially on the occasion of the wedding of the only woman he thought might actually have loved him.

The only woman he could now socialize with was his mother. He didn't seem to like being in her company, but something compelled him to be with her, a coercive force like a sword aimed at his throat. The time he spent chatting with her was full of reproach and muffled arguments. He would remind her of how cruelly she had treated him when he was young, the painful blows he had received from her. She didn't like his constant reminders. "Can't you forget? Rehashing the past does no good now. Let bygones be bygones."

He could never forget her cruelty. Had she not been his own mother, he would have deserted her and finally closed his heart to all women in an effort to avenge himself. His dialogue with her revealed this deep-seated resentment of women; it surfaced in his speech, which often ended in that tone of stifled tears. But he kept going back to try to make peace with her, his bitter chest filled with anger at the woman whom God had asked him to respect and humor, a woman who had never done anything for him. But the sheikhs always said, "Your mother, then your mother, then your mother. She carried you in weakness upon weakness."[52]

Deep down, he knew the "weakness" would be forgotten; he still remembered the day he leaned his back, sore from her beating, against the wall and asked 'Awatif, "Doesn't anyone love me in this house? I'm just a boy! What did I do?"

'Awatif was closest to him in age; she felt for him and played with him to make him feel better. But she grew up to fight with him like everyone else. The discord between them worsened when he saw that she, too, had turned out to be like all the girls of her generation—spoiled and impressed by everything they heard about women in the West, including their false freedom. Having surrendered to all the current waves of fashion and the new colonial invasion, she wore makeup like a Western girl, dressed up in revealing clothes, cut her hair short, and listened to music. And she didn't stop at that. She turned into his worst enemy, even worse than the infidel West! Every time he suggested she mend her ways, since she had been the only one who pitied him and whom he loved, she flew in his face: "You are backward! You have the mind of a medieval man!"

Ibrahim had been looking for a heart to cherish him when Jawza' showed him her love. He did suggest to my mother that he wanted to marry her, but she thought he was joking.

"Where will you live? Who will support you?" she asked him to complicate the issue.

---

52. In this saying, the Prophet Mohammed asserts his belief that a mother must be given priority above all other people in her children's affection and care. The "weakness" refers to the hardships a woman suffers when carrying, delivering, and rearing a child.

"I'll live with you; my father is obligated to maintain me as long as I live in his house. I want to keep myself chaste."

Mother refused to let him marry before he finished university, especially since he was intelligent and scored excellent grades. Ibrahim chose Islamic studies, the only major that came with a heavenly reward. Those who studied medicine or the humanities, he thought, were in it for worldly purposes—money and prestige—rather than the sheer love of God.

Every day he brought home flyers and pamphlets extolling the behavior of the ideal Muslim. Most urged young men to rescue their brothers in Afghanistan and enact the sixth obligation in Islam, which is jihad.

He also brought numerous Islamic tapes for my mother, asking her to share them with us and with her female neighbors. "These should be handed out for free in the streets, department stores, supermarkets, and wedding halls."

We had seen the flyers and pamphlets at school and university, at medical clinics and dispensaries, and even at amusement parks. Some of them had contest questions promising prizes such as cars and expensive electronics.

Twenty

IBRAHIM DID NOT COME HOME during the final exams of his first year at university for Islamic studies. We thought he had gone to one of his student camps, but Mother remained worried. She called Mansur, who promised to see her after the *'isha*[53] prayer.

Mansur's dark countenance reminded me of his old habits—and all the situations that made his features dull and lifeless. He talked to Mother about Ibrahim's disappearance. "He went to Pakistan, Aunt. The passport section at the airport confirmed it. And Pakistan is usually a stop on the way to Afghanistan."

My mother put her hands to her head; an anguished sound came from her chest. "May Allah protect us!"

Ammousha peered from the holes of her burka and asked Mansur, "Why should he go to Pakistan? Did he go to study or find a job?"

"No, Aunt Ammousha," replied Mansur. "He went to fight on the side of the Afghanis."

Ammousha missed all but the words "went to fight." She cried as she struck her head. "May Allah help us! Why fight? Is there a war coming to our land and he went to meet the armies there? Where did he go? Why did he leave his mother and sisters? *Hasbi Allah wahwa ni'ma l-wakeel!*"[54]

Ibrahim came back from Afghanistan six months later. He had become inscrutable, more sullen, more antisocial. We, his sisters, avoided him and hid in our rooms as soon as we came home. We used neither the

---

53. This is the evening prayer, the last prayer of the day.
54. This statement, which means "Allah is sufficient for me and is the best trustee of affairs," is usually uttered when one is facing a problem or has been wronged.

tape player nor the telephone to spare ourselves battles that would always end with beatings and torn hair, battles that would not quell our rebellion but would just make us bleed and send our mother to the clinic the next morning for hypertension.

He was no longer willing to sit around with Mother and Ammousha as he had in former days; he went off to the men's sitting room, to read or watch al-Jazeera and make mysterious phone calls. He stored cardboard boxes in the dining room, which no one used, and kept the key in his pocket.

Late one night, the doorbell rang. Ibrahim picked up the phone to the outside door and asked, "Who is it?"

He answered the door and came back with a man who took all the boxes from his room. Then the man removed everything Ibrahim had stored in the dining room, his secret storage place. Ibrahim cleaned it thoroughly and left it open before disappearing after the dawn prayer.

Freedom wafted into our home. Little Mae asked, "Mama, is Uncle Ibrahim coming back?"

"Only God knows. Why do you ask?"

"I don't want him to come back, Mama. He hates my toys. He breaks their necks wherever he finds them. He's a big man. Why does he hate children's toys?"

Twenty One

THE MORNING WAS unusually quiet. I missed the smell of coffee. It was my custom to have the smell slip its fingers into my hair, caress my cheek, and tickle my toes upon waking.

When I wake up, coffee receives me like the smiling face of a mother glad to be blessed with a child. "Good morning," I hear it say. The smell is always enough to make me feel that all is right with the world.

I left my room and was received only by the gloom that had settled on the house since the day we had last seen Ibrahim. To my mother, the house had become a hell empty of men. There were only women around, and these women lived alone, without a man to guard them. She started to take bigger doses of medication in order to keep her diabetes under control.

I found her sitting on her prayer mat reading the Qur'an. "Where are the girls?" I asked her.

"They went to school."

"This early?"

"You are late; it's seven thirty."

"Where's the coffee?"

"We didn't make coffee. I am fasting."

I was surprised to hear this. It was Wednesday, not a regular fasting day, not a Thursday or a Monday; nor was it one of the white days[55] in every month or the six days of Shawwal.[56]

---

55. Fasting three days of every month in the Hijri calendar (the Islamic lunar calendar), preferably the 13th, 14th, and 15th, is a Sunna, not obligatory, practice for Muslims.

56. Fasting six days of the Hijri month of Shawwal, after the three days of Eid al-Fitr, the feast

"Why are you fasting?" I asked.

"Penance."

"Penance for what?" I said laughing. "Did you take an oath and go back on it?"

"No, but twenty years ago I gave birth to a child called Mohammed. I was nursing him one night, during the early days of confinement, when I slept. I found him dead under my breast when I woke up."

"I know this story. It happened so long ago. Why do you remember it now?"

"It scares me to think that I was the one who killed the baby. Today I'll start a two-month fast to atone for it."

"Why now?"

"In the past I tended to believe what people said, that the death of infants during sleep was natural. But when I heard what one of the sheikhs had to say on TV, I got scared thinking that I was the one who caused the baby's death. Feelings of guilt won't leave me."

I left my mother and went to work wondering about what she said. Did she want to heal the old wound, or did she intend to punish herself for what had happened to Ibrahim?

At the hospital, a nurse called me. A patient was bleeding from the uterus and needed surgery. The staff in charge had called her husband but got no response. The patient's situation was getting critical.

"Why don't you take her to the operating room?" I asked.

"Her husband must sign the consent form. These are the rules."

"Has the patient herself agreed to have the surgery?"

"I don't know."

I went to her room. The woman was forty years old and suffering from abdominal pain. "Has the doctor talked to you about your condition?"

"Yes."

"Did he say you needed surgery?"

"Yes."

"Do you agree to have it?"

"Yes."

---

that immediately follows the fasting month of Ramadan, is another Sunna practice recommended by the Prophet Mohammed.

"Will you sign this form?"

"Yes."

I went out to tell the nurse that the patient was in agreement.

The file clerk, who stood near the desk, said, "The consent must come from her guardian."

"But he's not responding, and her condition may get worse. Besides, she is forty. Can't she be responsible for her own decision?"

"I know, but who would be responsible if her husband showed up here and didn't like the situation?"

"Aren't we in a government organization? Don't I, as a specialist in social work, represent the patient?"

"Will you sign to take responsibility?"

"Yes, I'll sign. Give me the patient's file."

I took the file to the patient, and when she signed the agreement form, I signed below her signature.

They took the patient to the operating room, while I kept calling her husband and getting no response.

Later, Shaza told me that she planned to join her family the next day, a Thursday, on a camping trip. Would I like to go with her?

"I don't know," I said. "Mother may object to the idea."

"Tell her that you have to work tomorrow,[57] and I'll pass by your place to pick you up at eight.

"Okay. I'll think about it."

I tried to sleep to drive away thoughts of having to sneak out with Shaza the next morning. I'm too old for this kind of behavior. Besides, I have come to prefer confrontation and combat to evasiveness and running away. I think I am old enough not to dissemble and flee, signs of fear and guilt.

Mother has been very depressed since Ibrahim left home. He, too, has let her down and gone away. Instead of fighting on her side, he went to fight in Afghanistan. No one wants to bear her banner; each prefers to bear his own.

Her illness and mental condition did not help me as I considered

---

57. At the time this story was set, Thursdays and Fridays were "weekend" days for schools and many government offices in Saudi Arabia.

fighting for the camping trip. Mother thinks life has already turned its back and Judgment Day is close at hand. People, therefore, should not be happy about anything. If she finds out that this kind of thinking has no effect on me, she will accuse me of being selfish, for my heart still enjoys going out and having a good time while my brothers are absent.

I will not fight with my mother while she is frail and sad. Valiant warriors don't play false, nor do they fight with the weak. But my heart is also weak, yearning for Waleed and longing to be with him. It beats like a caged bird, clapping its wings and hoping that I will open the door and let it fly to where he is.

In the evening I fought the desire to go camping with Shaza, even if it meant I wouldn't see Waleed. Yet every time I turned my back to my heart, it poked me like a persistent, tireless child. I rolled onto my left side when I heard the rattling swords of desire as its troops steadily marched toward me, demanding a fight or a surrender.

I tried to get in touch with Waleed. A recorded voice said, "The number you have dialed is temporarily out of service. Please call later. Thank you."

I texted him: "Where are you, my love?" I pressed Send and put my mobile phone on the bedside table. The bird inside me had just begun to calm down, somewhat relieved of the burden of desire, when the melody of a received message chimed twice. It was him: "I'm waiting for you at the campground. Come."

No sooner had I read his words than my heart's bird opened the door to its cage and flew. I decided to follow it in the morning.

Twenty Two

CLOUDS WERE MASSING over Najd's al-'Arid Mountains as the last days of winter bid farewell, promising an early spring. March is rarely forgotten by the rain. In our country rain is not a frequent visitor, but when it comes, it brings both joy and sorrow.

Memories evoked by the rain taste odd, bruising my heart and stirring regret for the years of my life I never fully lived. Strange are the feelings that rain excites: intoxicating delight, yet in the midst of joy you wonder, "What gives pleasure this taste of grief?"

On one side of the asphalt road, small flowers dotted the ground, and water drops shimmered like silver beads over the wild land. The earth had imbibed so much rain the previous night that it emitted a moist glow. On the road, traffic was light. Some cars carried coolers of food; they, too, were heading for the spring camping grounds.

The desert was baring her heart to all her children who had fled the city's oppressive hand, priming herself for their arrival like a bride decked in all sorts of colors: blue sky, white clouds, violet sands, the golden bangles of a veiled sun, and the green of one tree slipping its fingers into the hair of another tree.

On our way, the sun came out, lazy and smiling, as if a hand had roused her from a good night's sleep. Along one side of the Thamama road colorful tents lined up against enchanting dunes; on the other side the Tuwaiq Mountains loomed large, cleaving the heart of Najd from the east to the north. Water sparkled on the surface of the rocks we could see from the car windows. Below, the spongy sand looked radiant, having received plenty of rain. The sun shone on higher hills, making the sand hide the rain under its smooth skin. To reach the moisture, the sun must slip its fingers right under the dewy surfaces.

Waleed came out of the tent to welcome us, a blush of joy brightening his smile as he saw us. The cloak of camel hair over his shoulders reminded me of Grandfather Abdul-Muhsin, Selma's ardent lover. Waleed had worn a red *ghutra*[58] with its corners tied around his face. From the tent's door, he whispered to me, "Hello! The world is suddenly bright!"

After dinner, we got into the Japanese-made Jeep. Waleed switched on the Magellan device and a map came up on its screen, where the tent was marked as a black dot. "Look here," he told Shaza. "This is where we are. I've saved it here. And this black line is the road you will be taking. On the way back, you need to follow the black line to get to our starting point. Do you know how it works?"

"I know. Let me drive now."

Shaza drove us around to explore the area.

"Stop here," Waleed said.

He and I got out. Shaza said, "I'm going to drive up and down the sand hills, like we did when we were teenagers."

"All right, but make sure you save our spot on the Magellan so that you don't get us lost."

"Don't worry! You have a man here!" Shaza said, pounding on her chest and driving away.

The area was full of rocks. At one time, Waleed said, it had been a dam built on a large stream. With him beside me, I couldn't tell history from geography. Neither time nor place appeared to be what it was. I found myself in a timeless pendulum that swung between the past and the future. Now and then Waleed would bring me back to the present as he held my waist to kiss me.

"Hey, we're here!"

The earth glistened with springs, blue and brimming, shimmering like individual mirrors all around us. Who would believe that such colors, such water could be found in the heart of the Najdi desert?

Everything there breathed and whispered its own presence: the rocks,

---

58. A large square headdress worn by Arab men, with or without the '*iqal* (a double circle of black rope) to keep it in place.

the water, the mountains. The desert painted in a most detailed scene. It looked so real. We were the shadows. Never before had I encountered such an equation of nature on earth. Toward the horizon, the silent rocks, plants, and valley were revealed. The stone dam towering behind us had been built by hands that no longer existed. The more we walked the smaller we felt in the vast and infinite silence. We turned into little dots, tiny brown pebbles. Earth's quiet hues predominated everywhere, sublime and imposing.

Waleed ran his fingers through my hair; then he turned me toward him. He opened his brown cloak and, pulling me inside it, he pressed my body tightly to his. Like the sorceress in Najdi tales, I entered a tree trunk and flew away. I soared so high I could almost see the Garden of Eden lying below. My heart was racing: Was it fear or joy? No way of knowing. In my Eden, which opened its gate to take us inside, I was aware of a boundless space, which we viewed with eagle eyes, unobstructed by either the horizon or the distant mountains. Water from the night's rain trickled across the rocky floor under our feet. It was louder than all other sounds, acting like a bold man wandering around his own house and feeling proud of his domain, as if his pride, like the moist earth, would never go dry; a little girl was following him, happily playing, unperturbed by the heat of the sun on the day to come. The creatures around us expressed themselves with endless energy, whereas the presence of past human existence was hardly felt: few traces of those who had passed by this spot; they had played, traded, loved, married, procreated, fought, and cried, but in the end they went away, disappeared, died, leaving a remnant of their secrets on this earth. The spring no longer refreshed them.

I felt as if someone had lifted me up and turned me into air. My heart chirped with joy. I wanted to ask him whether he felt as light as I did, but I couldn't speak. Waleed's hands carried me away, and he burned me with fiery kisses that tortured my love-starved soul.

He gave me his hand to lift me out of the sand swing. I smoothed my dress and shook off the sand as my heart swooped down from its skies like a bird touching the ground while its wings still beat in the air. Waleed's hand sent the fever of existence into my body, which lost its lightness as gravity pulled it down. I felt my feet hit the ground, like a person returning from a dream or a Sufi nirvana.

"Did you feel something?" I asked Waleed.

"Yes. Exactly what you felt."

The light breeze blew the fig leaves out of my heart, revealing my passion for him. His eyes, fringed by dense eyelashes, looked at me with tenderness and love, black irises floating in a happy and serene white. It was the gaze of someone entreating God to grant him an impossible dream. He smiled as he looked at me under the sun; he could see how deeply I was in love with him. I said, "I always have the feeling that life doesn't offer itself wholly to us; it gives us only half of the happiness we need, and we're left to deal with misery for the other half. Kazantzakis once said something to that effect. He was visiting Athens, a city that filled him with wonder and joy. Nevertheless, he felt that the devils were watching him, lying in wait for him. Since he believed that happiness didn't come without a price, he rushed to the market and bought a pair of tight shoes, intended to squeeze his feet and make them hurt while he wandered around the city. He preferred to pay a price he knew for the happiness he lived, instead of waiting for a random price to fall on his head."

Waleed laughed to hear me say that. He playfully said, "Then he was the one who punished himself, not God!"

"How awful, Waleed; you've spoiled a beautiful picture with your realism."

He laughed again at my simplicity. "Who taught you to think it's right to enjoy pain? You're like my sister, Shaza, in this regard. This is called masochism. God would never run after you with a whip in his hand! Why do you bother about watching your slip ups? You are a wonderful woman, Hend, and all you do expresses this. Has anyone told you the opposite?"

"No one has ever told me I am wonderful! My mother always thought her daughters were the reason for her troubles and sleepless nights. Mansur assigned me to a class he called *hareem*, deficient in both intellect and religious principles. And Ibrahim eyed me with fear, as though I were Satan himself. Even my father! He looked at me with pitying eyes, as though I were a wounded bird that would always need a cage to keep the cats from eating it. Why do you think I shouldn't view myself as guilty?"

"But I see you as a brilliant woman! Are you listening to what I say? Always remember that."

"Only *you* think I am an independent woman who can think and talk and love. The brilliance you see is your image in my mirror, when my mirror is very clear."

Twenty Three

MY MIDDLE SISTER, Mashael, came to visit us. She had doted on me like no one else. I was both her sister and friend. We played together, cooked together, and got punished together. She kept my secrets from our mother and paid for errors she didn't commit. It was hard for Mother to believe that Mashael knew nothing about what I did; the fact that I was at fault was enough to get her in trouble. Mashael had married one of our relatives whom she had grown to love through correspondence, for which she was hounded by guilt. Every day her religion teacher reminded the class that God would not be lenient with those who follow Satan's schemes of love and passion, for love is nothing but a snare that leads young girls to unwed pregnancy. Therefore, Mashael married her pen lover while in her first year of secondary school and then stayed at home busying herself with a life of perpetual pregnancy and childbirth. In seven years she had six children. Her husband believes that contraceptives go against religion, that a fertile woman is evidence of a sound bed and a sturdy womb, and that God will provide for the children. Mashael visits only on Thursdays, wearing black gloves and black socks, her face looking permanently tired. Her children are demanding, but she is afraid that if she fails to meet their demands or her husband's, he will marry another woman. She feels sorry for us, 'Awatif and me, for we are lost in sin and far removed from God's mercy. Angels fear to enter our rooms, which are full of pictures, figures, and songs.

This time she brought a lifeboat for me, one that she thought would keep me safe and put me on the right track. Mother provided the first thread of the conversation: "Mashael has a bridegroom for you."

My mobile rang. I left the living room to answer it. Waleed was on the line.

"I'm going to the airport, and I wanted to hear your voice before I fly."

"I'll e-mail you. Take care of yourself."

I went back to the living room. Mashael was silent, but my mother said, "Captain Badr, a friend of Mashael's husband, wants to marry you. His wife can't have children, and he asked for your hand."

It seemed that my mother would never surrender. She had now decided to lead a new sally against me and must enlist the help of a captain. "Does his eminence, the captain, know that I work at the hospital?"

"What do you need this work for after your marriage? Besides, the man wants children, meaning that you will be busy with kids."

I gave Mashael a menacing look. She turned her head and occupied herself with nursing her baby. 'Awatif rushed in while ending a mobile call. "Switch on the TV," she said. "The General Security building was bombed!"

The TV showed pictures of the recent destruction to some of the building's levels: glass everywhere, people beginning to crowd the scene, dense smoke rising to the sky, and vehicles from the Civil Defense filling the area.

"May Allah guide them to the right path," Mashael said.

'Awatif gasped, turning to her: "May Allah blast them and relieve us of their presence!"

"Don't curse them; they are Muslims! It is not right to curse them; just pray for Allah's guidance," said Mashael.

I gave Mashael a baffled look.

"Baba's picture!" Mae cried.

Mansur, who works at the General Security building, appeared on the screen in his military clothes. He was injured and receiving treatment. Mae was jumping up and down frantically. "Why is Baba bleeding from his neck?" she cried, hitting me on the shoulder. I took her hand and ran with her away from the scene.

"Don't worry, darling; your father will be fine."

I called Mansur, but his mobile was switched off.

Mae continued to cry. Mother came in rubbing her hands.

"Hasbi Allah wahwa ni'ma l-wakeel. Call one of his brothers; they must be near him."

I dialed his brother Mohammed, who answered my call. "Is Mansur all right?"

"Yes, he's all right. We are with him at the hospital. He was wounded in the neck but his condition is stable. Don't worry; it's nothing serious."

"Could he speak to his daughter? She's almost falling apart!"

"Fine, no problem. Give her the phone."

"Baba, are you dying?" Mae screamed. . . . "Okay, Baba!" She ended the call.

"Baba is coming," she said. "He'll take me with him."

She went to put her clothes in a bag and waited for him till she was overcome by sleep.

In the early morning, the doorbell rang. Mae ran out to the door and came back. "Baba's here!"

My heart sank. I heard my mother say, "*Inna llillah wa inna ilayhi raji'oon.*"[59]

Mansur came in; the side of his neck was covered with a piece of gauze. Mae brought her bag and sat next to him, unwilling to leave his side. She decided to guard her father against death. "I will stay with you, Baba; I will never let you die."

Mansur kissed her hand, his eyes glistening with tears. He asked my mother to go with him to the men's sitting room for a private talk.

When my mother came back, her eyes were also wet with tears. She went to her room and returned with a suitcase. Mansur said, "I'm taking Mae and Aunt Heila to our village in al-Zulfi. They should be kept away from bad news. Aunt's health cannot take bad news."

"Is there anything worse than this?"

"God help us."

'Awatif tagged along with them, Ammousha went to her own village, and I took my suitcase and left.

I, too, had decided to leave. My mother had talked with Fahad about my new suitor, Captain Badr. She wanted him to talk me into marrying the man. After all, I was now a divorced woman, so my prospects extended only to being a second wife or the wife of an old widower.

---

59. To Allah we belong and to him we return.

Fahad convinced her to let me visit him, explaining that he would be able to reason with me if we were together away from Riyadh; then, he said, he would come home with me for the wedding. Mother was ready to do anything Fahad asked just so that I would consent to have her new soldier for a husband. She believed what Fahad said about winning me over and returning with me to Riyadh. She thought she would be happy twice over: with his return and my marriage. All this will happen! It must happen! She had no choice but to believe him. Mother would not be reconciled to the absence of her sons. Things must fall back into their rightful place, as she herself had planned. And in the absence of his father, Fahad would stay home to guard over his female dependents. He would also give his sister in marriage. Ibrahim, too, would come back home, get married, and live with the family. I myself would move out to be with my husband, whom I would complain about quite a lot. But a woman is more submissive in her second married life; her position is so much weaker, forcing her to be more lenient, more resigned; a marriage is not a dress, to be easily discarded. She let me go to Canada.

For his part, Fahad listened to what I had to say. He gave in to my pleas for help just this once.

"Do you want to leave the country so that you can run away with him?" he asked.

"No, I will not run away, I promise you. But I would like to have the chance to know Waleed better—away from the hell of sins I have around me everywhere. I no longer know if he is heaven or hell. I just want to know him better so that I don't involve myself in a relationship that will end up like the one I had with Mansur."

"Okay."

Fahad was convinced; he agreed to come to my rescue. For the first time he was willing to undertake some of the family responsibilities that he'd always managed to avoid.

Twenty Four

_࿇_

IN THE SUMMER Riyadh turns into a very large oven pumping fire from all directions into the motionless air. The sky assumes a dusty countenance, a rather alarming crimson face, at dawn. By noon, the outside walls are hot to the touch, and all you hear, all day long, is air conditioners laboring for breath. People drink ice-cold water, lie down in the cool air, and shut their minds to all attempts to make them face the heat. Some turn sluggish and cranky, even violent and aggressive. Young men trade insults and gesture rudely at each other, and fights erupt that shock the nerves. The heat pushes people out of the temperament they had back in the winter. Just imagine an outage in one of the city's tall buildings! The horrors of a Hitchcock film! Thinking of the summer's heat squeezing my mind, I gasped for a moment.

The driver asked: "Do airplanes manage to fly in this weather? It's almost impossible to see."

Strange red hues darkened the sky and dimmed the lights. We stopped at a roadblock, where police had parked and were demanding drivers' IDs.

I asked the driver to switch off the radio, which was airing a frivolous song.

Four motorcycles zoomed by, four young Saudi men aboard. Seconds later a police car raced past, followed by three others.

Police vehicles blocked the western exits of the roundabout leading to the airport; it seemed that a police chase was in progress. Such scenes were now very common in Riyadh. Only the night before, al-Arabia and al-Jazeera had both showed a picture of Johnson, the American man, his head severed from his body. The man had been kidnapped and killed by al-Qaeda members in Riyadh in retaliation for the murder of Abdul Aziz al-Muqrin, the head of al-Qaeda in the city. Hideous scenes like these were no longer banned; satellite channels competed to broadcast them.

I stood before the passport personnel holding a document authorizing my trip, which Mansur had prepared for me the night before. The official didn't pay much attention to the name; he just made sure the paper was authentic. Women running away from Riyadh no longer represented a major problem in the minds of inspectors. They were too busy looking for terrorists. I walked into the cool airport, its marble floor glittering as though someone had poured water over it. It fooled the eye the way Balqis's eye had been tricked the day she met the Prophet Solomon.[60]

One of the stories suggests that he wanted to assure himself about the shape of her feet, which had been rumored to be the hooves of a goat.[61] Why is it that a woman's feet are central to myths? I walked along the railing of the upper hallways, delighted to see the water fountains flowing among planted trees in the open space inside the airport. Perhaps it was the idea of traveling that lifted my spirits.

Flights and boarding announcements turned the airport into an external planet, orbiting outside family and home: a spaceship is bound to come along and take us on board. I look at the time for Riyadh and for Toronto, where I will be. My heart follows the clock of its new location.

Planes following international routes spread their wings to carry people almost everywhere in the world. The airport and Riyadh seemed to be in totally different time zones. Here I sit midway between the city and the outside world, no longer crammed inside Riyadh's black abaya or its streets; I have moved into a sphere where time is compressed, where people handle high-precision technical equipment with laser beams, computer screens, and wireless devices. Everything here is subject to accurate measures; there is no room for carelessness or sloth.

---

60. According to the Qur'anic tale, when Balqis, Queen of Saba', entered the Prophet Solomon's house, she bared her legs thinking that she was going to wade in water. She did not know that the floor had been built of glass, using the latest technology of the time.

61. This part of the story is not mentioned in the Qur'an but has since been added to the tale.

The cool and solemn waiting area breathed into my face and brought me back from my recent excursion into space. A new sense of being alive was stirring inside me.

I picked up a few newspapers from a rack in a duty-free shop; I also had a cup of coffee, whose heady smell woke up the lethargic pathways in my head.

I opened *Al-Sharq al-Awsat*,[62] which showed, like all other newspapers, pictures and analyses of the latest terrorist act. Images of those who had carried it out covered the paper's first page: youthful faces, newly killed, their names printed too close together. Among them was a clean-shaven youth with abundant hair. My heart held on to his image. I knew this face: the high nose, like that of a Greek warrior; the long black hair, like that of Che Guevara, the obstinate rebel; and the eyes, which now closed their lids in everlasting rest. Some of his face was covered with blood. A violent blow struck my gut. I knew this face very well. The waiting room was getting colder, squeezing my stomach. My eyes were chasing black flies . . . I knew these features, but the blood covering them made me think I had a problem concentrating, the type I encounter in my nightmares. Was it day or night? I couldn't quite tell. I used my hand to drive away the black flies before my eyes. They didn't go; they buzzed in my ears while I tried to be sure I knew the face. He was clean-shaven today, but his features I have known since I was a young girl. Ibrahim, my brother Ibrahim! Another kick to my stomach! I was choking on the fluids rising to my throat when I ran to the nearest bathroom. I sank onto the toilet closest to the door.

I don't know how much time I spent on the seat with saliva running down my hand, sour fluids burning my throat, and stinging tears flowing from my eyes. I got up to wash my face at the sink. The cold water brought me back to sordid reality. I looked in the mirror but didn't see my face; I saw his instead, Ibrahim's beardless face, blood staining his features and hair, eyes closed, dreaming of a peace he had never tasted in life.

My body collapsed once again. I found myself shivering under the

---

62. *The Middle East.*

marble sink. Fresh tears came to my eyes as I wrapped my arms across my chest.

Images that I couldn't control darted through my consciousness; I was like someone watching a black-and-white Egyptian movie with handkerchief in hand, watching and wiping off the tears: Ibrahim's face as a child, crying because my mother hit him; Ibrahim in tears as my father drags him out; his voice coming from the mosque's loud speakers, reading a homily; his words as he leans his sore back against the wall: "Doesn't anyone love me in this house?" Then comes his figure standing against our door, smiling as he watches Jawza', followed by the sound of water in the bathroom, where he washes away his sins.

I recalled how close we were as children and how he had turned into a stranger when he grew up. Mansur must have known about Ibrahim's involvement in the event before any of us did; that must be why he seemed so gentle, taking Mother along with him to al-Zulfi and letting me travel abroad without creating any obstacles.

So many questions accompanied my tears: Why did he leave us to go away? Why did he do it? Was it because he believed no one in the family cared for him? Who in the family really loved him? But whom did he love that didn't reciprocate his affection? Did he think that this cruel, loveless world deserved a ruthless counterattack? Or did he want to prove he belonged to it by showing himself equally heartless?

Painful sensations hard to identify coursed through my body. My heart ached with pity and sorrow. For the first time I felt tender toward Ibrahim, unhappy for parting with him, and fully aware of the loneliness he must have felt taking the road he chose for himself. I had now a greater desire to flee the nightmare of our existence. Inside me, too, there was a woman ready to wrap herself with bombs, to blow up her body, to lay down the burdens she carried in a scene she wanted to end, either by death or by departure.

The final call came for boarding the plane. I was freezing. The low temperatures in the airport made the place feel like a morgue. The soldiers' boots continued to pound the airport floor. A glass door was rising between me and everyone else: I could see them but couldn't sense their humanity in a place that felt like a wax museum.

A security officer dressed in the airport uniform stood over my head. "Are you flying to Toronto?" he asked.

My heart throbbed as I heard him say the words; I didn't have a ready answer. I thought of going back home. But my mother couldn't have heard the news. Mansur would keep it from her. The man saw the tears frozen on my cheeks.

"I hope you're all right," he said. "Is something bothering you?"

"No."

"Are you ready for the trip?"

That was the question I needed to hear to grab the safety rope that came dangling from the sky.

"Yes, ready."

"Come on then. Your papers, please."

I gave him all my papers; fear was raising the temperature of my body.

"No, just your plane ticket."

He tore the ticket in two and gave me one part.

"Please," he said, motioning me in.

The smell of travel wafted by; I knew it well. I don't know how, but as soon as my body smells it, my arms begin to shake off their weight and sprout black feathers, long and soft, right where the cold air has left its goosebumps. I hear them beating, like the wings of a dove. My body, too, shakes off its weight, going against the earth's gravity. I glide through the long passage between the seats, like a bird gliding in space, heedless of those who stare or note its presence.

Quietly, the plane moved. It was seven in the morning, the hour's first minute ticking away on my watch, marking its passage from the last morning in Riyadh and into the first morning in the sky. With its doors tightly shut, the metallic plane turned into a white bird soon to be rising to the sky with one last call from its captain. My lap felt the tightening of the seatbelt, and my legs dangled a little as the plane left the ground. It was like being on an amusement park ride: tickling sensations spread through my stomach and light air filled my lungs as my soul laid down its weight and let me fly. I put one of the seat's earphones to my ear; one channel was playing Mohammed Abdu's song "Riyadh's Face Graced My Eyes."

The flight attendant pointed at the pot in her hand: "Coffee?"

I smiled through my tears, nodding my head as I swallowed my grief for my brother, myself, and my mother. I took the first sip of my first coffee in the first sky as I heard Mohammed Abdu singing the praises of Riyadh: "Her palm unraveling the braid of words . . ."

An Interview with Badriah Albeshr

An Interview with Badriah Albeshr

CONDUCTED BY SANNA DHAHIR

THIS IS A TRANSLATION of an interview that took place on March 26, 2013, in Dubai, where I met the author at one of her favorite cafés. The interview was part of a research-based course I taught in 2013, which involved interviewing five prominent Saudi writers. Many of the questions below were provided by my students, who had read the Arabic version of *Hend and the Soldiers* and were curious to know more about the writer, her characters, and her beliefs.

Looking elegant in a long skirt and a blouse, Albeshr was very relaxed and welcoming. We sat in one of the corners of the café, and after a few comments about the nice weather, I told her about my class project. "Let me hear your students' questions," she said, smiling, and we started talking about her life and writings.

Q. This question is personal: How did you meet your husband, the comedy star Nassir Alqassabi? (Albeshr is well known for being married to Nassir Alqassabi, and my students were particularly interested in this aspect of her life.)

A. That is quite a story. I was a student at King Saud University at the time, and my friends and I were working on a project to showcase at the end-of-year celebrations. We were planning to put on a short play about the problems of schoolwork, and we thought of calling Nassir to ask him if he could help us by writing a comic scene about the problems we had in mind. When I phoned him, he was obliging, but not prompt. He wanted to know more about the problems that we faced as students, and the time it took to go over the details gave us the chance to get to know each other.

I was surprised a month later when he said that he was ready to write the scene if I consented to marry him. I thought at first he was joking, so I said, "Fine, finish the scene and I'll marry you." I never thought this was going to be real. I took some time to think about this proposal because I thought it might not be easy to become an actor's wife. Then I thought why not, and the whole thing turned out to be much simpler than I had expected.

Q. How long have you been in Dubai? Do you prefer living here to living in Saudi Arabia?

A. I have been here since 2006. And I prefer to live here. The life I lead in Dubai suits me better as a writer. I am a woman who likes to wake up early in the morning, go to the gym, and then sit in a café to write over a cup of coffee. My ability to leave the house and separate myself from my home life is very important to my career. Again, my presence among people of different genders makes me feel emotionally secure, something that I need as a writer. Dubai is a peaceful city; people here are a mixture of all nationalities and ethnic groups, and this is an indication of a peaceful coexistence, as well as variety and multiplicity, something that comforts the writer.

Q. Do you teach at a university here?

A. I was teaching here until two years back. My constant traveling made me realize I needed to assign some solid time for my writing, so I am now dedicated to my writing.

Q. In Hend wa-l-'Askar, our society's negative aspects are shown from the point of view of a woman. Are women better able to observe these shortcomings?

A. I have my reservations about the idea that what I wrote was a record of shortcomings. Literature is a human vision, which we all have. Some, for example, write about a war in Japan; others about hunger and misery in Russia. The writer's eye picks up these things. Women have gone through trying times in this world, and in Saudi Arabia as a part of it. Relentless traditions have alienated women from their own identities and prevented them from making free choices, and these issues are clear and obvious and tormenting. As a woman, I may not have experienced all these pains, but I have sensed all of them one way or another. Depicting social issues and writing about them makes them public. To be sure, women don't have more penetrating vision than men do. It is my belief that the creative writer, man or woman, has the ability to notice daily occurrences and turn them into a story or a poem. For example, *Madame Bovary* is one of the most poignant love stories and it shows a most painful struggle, but this is because the writer was creative. The issue has nothing to do with the sex of the writer.

Q. In the life of every Arab girl, there is a soldier, like the ones that surround Hend in your novel. Did your work as a university professor help you see similar examples?

A. Of course, the university has nothing but women, and it has provided me with the opportunity to create characters—in addition to my mother and grandmother and their neighbors and every other woman I have met, who all have stories that often repeat themselves. The army in their lives may not necessarily be men, for there are a lot of women who adopt the same views that oppose and restrain other women. These turn into soldiers, like Hend's mother, for example. They acquire the soldier's spirit that obeys without thinking, that commands with cruelty and without mercy. This military system may be suitable for a warfront but not for daily life, especially in family settings and among siblings and parents. I made sure to express this idea. Militarizing society in this way is the gist of the novel. It leads to emotional deprivation and it makes life dry—a bunch of strict rules that don't allow human beings in general to realize their individuality because it frowns upon differences. This militarism stems from a net of suffocating views that still controls university girls, as well as their mothers and other women.

Q. Saudi novels insist on investigating social problems, something that has started to irritate young women, who usually look for fictional worlds different from their own. How do you respond to this?

A. Readers are different, and they look for different things in a narrative. For example, when I was fifteen, I looked for "Abeer" books, the romantic love stories that target teenage girls. In my twenties, I was looking for novels that portrayed a spirit of rebellion, of struggle, and of youthful vigor. The Syrian poet Nizar Qabbani appealed to me for this reason. In my thirties, I was looking for philosophical novels, such as those of Hermann Hesse and Kazantzakis. In my forties, I was fascinated by Kundera. And each reader is, by instinct, as well as by literary and emotional bent, looking for appealing reading materials. We can't expect the writer to satisfy all tastes or all needs; the writer is not a singer following the audience's demands. And even singers differ widely and have different audiences, as in Umm Kulthoum, Farid al-Atrash, and Amru Diab. Each writer has a specific style and specific messages, and for each reader there are specific favorite writers.

Q. We as Saudis have been criticized as a nation lacking freedom of expression. As a constructive Saudi writer, what do you think of this comment?

A. I believe that the lack of freedom of expression is a problem in the whole Arab world. It's a problem especially in developing societies. However, it's important that we know how vital it is to have the freedom to be able to voice our own ideas. It gives us the chance to show how different we are from others. In the absence of this freedom, we say and hear the same thing, and when the ceiling of freedom is so low, life fails to provide the chance for uniqueness or individualism. People tell the same stories and repeat the same things; they obey and submit. But self-expression is a human instinct, evident in ancient drawings, carvings, and wall writings. The freedom to express oneself is important not only for the creative writer but also for the journalist and the politician and all other humans. With it we can better assess who we were, what we are now, and what we want to be in the future.

Q. During the last fifteen years or so, Saudi society in some ways has started to open up to the outside world, and Saudi writers have experienced some freedom of expression, which was not there in the previous century. What are the reasons that have made people more receptive to new ideas and better able to deal with issues most earlier writers did not feel comfortable dealing with?

A. Change is a universal thing, and evidence of change can be seen everywhere on this earth. I did my PhD on globalism in the Gulf countries, and I tried to look at three main things that connect these countries with the outside world: the Internet, the mobile phone, and the media, especially satellite TV. I was thinking mostly about the new generation, brought up on Turkish and Latin American soap operas, and being aware that there are other worlds that are more flexible and that allow their citizens many more freedoms than does their own. The youth nowadays are being exposed to various sources of knowledge coming from all sides. It isn't easy to escape change. Don't forget that prosperity has made travel easier, to Dubai and Bahrain, if not to Europe and the States. Today, too, scholarship programs send thousands of Saudi students abroad to get their education. All this, undoubtedly, will create a generation that is different from the previous one, and this is progress, which is a good thing.

Q. This is a question you have partially addressed. In your writings, what are the audiences you usually target?

A. This is a question I ask myself, especially after I discovered that many other writers pay attention to the audience they write for. To whom do I write? I found that I care about two groups, women and the new generation, which are more receptive of my ideas. There are, however, some women (and men) who are set in their ways and don't care for change. To me this audience is hard to reach or influence; they have already made up their mind. I address university students, people between twenty and thirty. This age group is more open; they are on a journey of exploration. I do hope I provide an opportunity for discovery. It is hard, however, to limit the age of one's readers; one can only speak of this matter in general terms. It's important to have a wide and varied readership.

Q. Your style of writing is very engaging and flows smoothly and freely. You also write as a woman, and you don't seem to mimic the traditional style of those who came before you, male or female. How did you develop your style?

A. Writing is something instinctive. But as a beginner, I mimicked other writers, like a child mimicking her mother—high heels and lipstick—and pretending to be someone else. But with time, practice, and the real desire to be creative, I started to find my own writing style in the mid-1980s. I am someone who is traveling on a long road, and each time I come across something that deserves to be owned, I put it in my bag. This bag has become richer. There was a time when I admired the elegant style of Lebanese writers. I also loved the modest Egyptian spirit that is so close to the street. And I liked Marquez's magical realism; I believe that it's truly a part of Eastern life. Anthropologists speak about the importance of myth and legend in people's lives, and when myth and magic exert influence on people's behavior, then they are a part of their reality, not to be treated as delusions or misconceptions. This realization showed me further dimensions of humanity. The woman who visits a saint's tomb so that she can bear a child is a woman performing an act that affects her life and energy, and this is, I think, a rich subject. Back to your question, the first story I ever wrote was titled "Rif'a"; in it I had a village girl (a village similar to my grandmother's) as the main character. This girl spends many hours of her day preparing herself to meet the man she loves near the village well, and she anxiously prepares for this encounter, washing her dress and borrowing a jewel from her mother, her heart pounding all day as she does the household chores and takes care of her mother's and brothers' needs. In the end her mother saddles her with the responsibility of calling on the neighbors. I was in my early twenties when I wrote this story, and I knew then that the story was mine, and I held on to this realization, proud that I was not just copying. I learned to be independent and persistent, something I inherited from my mother.

Q. Tell us about your mother. Was she like Hend's mother?

A. Quite, but my mother was a little more flexible. My mother worshipped traditions, but I haven't met many mothers of her generation who didn't. Actually, Hend's mother was born to me when I saw a woman in Lebanon beating her daughter in the vestibule of her house and cursing her in a loud voice. This suddenly reminded me of my mother's anger when I was late coming home, and I felt that most mothers are alike in their faithfulness to strict, draconian traditions. This faithfulness makes the daughter unable to understand her mother, and she always finds her to blame. Being faithful to traditions and sacrificing love for them is a trait shared by mothers, as well as fathers. I judged the mother harshly because she is of the same gender and has tasted the same bitterness in her life, but she still repeats this suffering.

Q. Hend's mother is very strong, but her strength hardly brings her close to the reader. Generally, one doesn't feel sympathy for her since she is against life and love and all that feeds the mind and soul. On the other hand, Hend's father is less strict and generally more sympathetic despite his cruelty toward his wife on their wedding night when she was no more than a child. What makes a woman adhere to traditions so strictly? Is it ignorance or is it the fear of stepping out of a circle drawn out for her by society?

A. I think that women like Hend's mother don't have a choice, mainly because their mothers did not exercise freedom of choice. Hend's generation, too, has been denied this freedom. Restricted as a female child, a woman turns into a victim of her upbringing, and when it is her turn to be a mother, she often uses the same disciplinary style. It's a training that breeds women's oppression. But perhaps mothers have no knowledge that this is cruelty. What do they know behind their closed doors? They think that safety is in staying inside the house. They find it hard to adventure out or give their daughters the chance to even open the door because what lies behind it is a scary world that a mother should not expose her daughter to. A woman's surrender to this massive amount of fear makes her cruel toward her daughter; those who see her think that she is a monster, but she is a human being terrified of what lies behind her closed door. Even today many women don't have choices. They have become frozen in time, for they must silence pain and questions and rebellion. In today's world, their insistence on being faithful to tradition makes them lose their identity as mothers. Each has become a chess figure in a game, not a human being leading a life inside her home. The same can be said about the father in the novel. He may be affectionate, but he assumes a male role when he subjugates his wife. Although he is a peaceful person, he understands that this woman is his possession and she must submit to him. This dilemma, the lack of familial understanding and love, begets nothing but an arid life, and everyone is a victim, even the sons.

Q. Yes, men, especially young men, in your writings have their own package of problems. Steering the ship is not as easy as some people may think. What are the things that make a man confused in a male-oriented society like ours? What are his own constraints?

A. Traditions, too. I believe that the strict traditions in the society which I have described as "military" are traditions that distance the man from his own self. He, too, functions according to a prefigured role. In particular, he should not be lenient in matters of honor, and he must always have the upper hand. He is not brought up to believe that life is a partnership, but hierarchical, with one person above another. Like women, men become alienated from themselves and their humanity, and women acquire a lower status in their eyes. In many families, even in recent times, a boy's hanging around his sisters, joking or laughing, is deemed shameful, as it is believed to dull the edge of his masculinity— all against common sense and the fact he is his mother's son and sister's brother, and that within the family setting of males and females, relationships ought to be built on understanding, and love and laughter. A man's estrangement from his real nature creates a problem for him, a problem of communicating with or understanding the women in his life. In this respect, he is no different from the woman who insists that her role is to surrender and submit. Both are victims of strict, predetermined rules.

Q. As you have explained, men and women suffer under traditional mores that limit their freedom and make life unbearable. How do you find our society now and what are the customs and conventions that Badriah Albeshr stands against?

A. Most conventions! Currently our society has many channels toward progress; important among these are the universities, such as Dar al-Hikma and Effat, and Prince Sultan and Al-Yamama, which have been providing education and advanced programs, more advanced than governmental education. Furthermore, I think that the Internet and social media have contributed to broadening the horizons of men and women and developing their awareness of other modes of living and thinking. In many families a woman, for example, is no longer the subdued person who accepts what others plan for her. All the instruments of knowledge in our life, I am sure, will create a more enlightened generation, one that will always clash with and argue against sterile conventions. I mean that the woman nowadays is no longer a person who subjects herself to prohibitions. She can choose the college major she wants, the man she wants to marry, the number of children she would like to have, and the career she wants to pursue. These are choices women in the past did not have; they were not available to the women in *Hend wa-l-'Askar*. Human beings are much freer when they have choices, and they can turn into slaves in the absence of these choices. The beliefs I most dislike are those that are dedicated to seeing women as incomplete, with a mind and abilities inferior to men's. Traditional thinking of this kind is not altered by the example of women like Merkel in Germany, or Hillary Clinton, America's foreign minister; nor is it defeated by the example of women who excelled in our history and were able to lead in different situations, women who craved and assumed power and sovereignty. The conventions that emphasize the shortcomings of women deprive them of free choice: in education, major, career, husband, and number of children. These traditions are against the humanity of a woman, and they are what I dislike most. I have written about such a convention in a story I called "The Ghost," in which a girl is being married to a young man who has asked for her hand in the traditional way. Throughout the engagement period she keeps thinking about what he will look like: her father? her brother? or someone on TV, whose work is like his (in the airlines)? She is looking for a ghost. On her wedding day, when he enters her field of vision, she sees first with her downcast eyes his brown shoes, then his socks, then his thobe; and when her eyes fall on his face, she finds that he resembles no one she knows; he is a stranger. A woman marrying a man she has never seen before is a kidnapping. It's inhuman to have a woman wed to a man whose voice she has never heard, whose face she has never seen, and with whom she has never talked. And in one night he becomes the person who is most intimate with her. This is unacceptable.

Q. Did you grow up in a family that encouraged reading and writing, or did you face problems similar to the ones faced by Hend?

A. I was born to parents who did not go to school, which means that books were not available to me until I was able to buy them in high school. At the same time, my family encouraged learning. They also loved folktales and folksongs. My grandmother was a first-rate storyteller and reciter of poetry. And there are women in my family who love to sing, and when they get together, they sing all kinds of folksongs and recall the occasions for which they were composed. In other words, these women created an oral theater. Although I chose the written word, the folk memory in my family was so rich that it left its impact on me. I have inherited the gene of storytelling.

Q. Who are the Arab and Western writers that influenced your thinking and writing?

A. I have a long list of writers and books. I started reading Naguib Mahfouz and Yusuf Idris and Nizar Qabbani and Ghada al-Samman, and then moved to reading translated books by Hemingway, Hermann Hesse, Kazantzakis, Faulkner, and Shakespeare. I mostly read novels and plays. Today I have formed my own literary family, with Isabel Allende as my mother, Marquez as my father, and Kundera as my uncle. I told myself long ago, since I couldn't choose my own biological family, I could choose my literary family, and I was happy with my filial relationship to Allende, whom I'll always call "mother," and my kinship to Virginia Woolf, my aunt, and with the companionship of all the brothers and relatives I chose to have. Every time I get attached to a new writer, I make him or her a member of my literary family.

Q. Your novel *Hend wa-l-'Askar* created an uproar and was met with scathing criticism when it first came out. Some writers publishing around the same time, the "chick-lit" writers in particular, were criticized as having deliberately created this reaction in order to attract attention to their work. Did you intend to do the same by writing this novel, as some readers have said?

A. No, of course not. No serious writer would deliberately choose to clash with the reader. When one writes a fictional work, one wants to express honest opinion, and the last thing the creative writer would want to do is to clash with the audience. However, when the writer realizes that the work is going to create some problems, I don't think they would choose to sacrifice their beliefs just to avoid these problems. Misunderstandings often occur, and this is what happened with my novel, for what I wrote in this novel, what people call "provocative" material, was no more than a small percentage of what other writers have published; but this novel was picked to be maligned by some groups who believed that it was to their advantage that they silence me. They chose to attack me in a very noisy way, using different methods to stir the emotions of those who don't use their minds but only submit to what is being said. I think what happened had more to do with a political game than with honest literary criticism. We can't judge literature in a legal court; we can't say this is halal and this haram. Do we punish an actor who kills another on the stage? In fiction we encounter the same thing. When characters utter words or commit acts that are unacceptable to some people, the writer does not necessarily believe in what they say or do. They are figures expressing themselves inside a book. It seems that attacking novels in the Arab world is a most successful way to have free advertisement for certain ideologies, and it works.

Lightning Source UK Ltd.
Milton Keynes UK
UKOW03f1134190517
301447UK00001B/54/P